Cat's Eye Corner

Cat's Eye Corner

By Terry Griggs

RAINCOAST BOOKS

Vancouver

Raincoast Books is a member of CANCOPY (Canadian Copyright
Licensing Agency). No part of this publication may be reproduced,
stored in a retrieval system or transmitted in any form or by any means
without prior written permission from the publisher, or, in case of
photocopying or other reprographic copying, a license from CANCOPY,
One Yonge Street, Toronto, Ontario, M5E 1E5.

Raincoast Books acknowledges the ongoing financial support of the
Government of Canada through The Canada Council for the Arts
and the Book Publishing Industry Development Program (BPIDP);
and the Government of British Columbia through the BC Arts Council.

Edited by Joy Gugeler
Typeset and cover design by Bamboo & Silk Design Inc.
Cover art and chapter illustrations by Cynthia Nugent

NATIONAL LIBRARY OF CANADA CATALOGUING IN PUBLICATION DATA

Griggs, Terry.
  Cat's eye corner

  ISBN 1-55192-350-5

  I. Title.
PS8563.R5365C37 2000   jC813'.54   C00-910707-X
PZ7.G8842Ca 2000

Library of Congress Catalogue Number: 2002092925

Raincoast Books   *In the United States:*
9050 Shaughnessy Street   Publishers Group West
Vancouver, British Columbia   1700 Fourth Street
Canada V6P 6E5   Berkeley, California
www.raincoast.com   94710

3 4 5 6 7 8 9 10

Printed in Canada by Webcom

JM son,
Sandy

TABLE OF CONTENTS

ONE

Cat's Eye Corner was full of rooms and rooms — cavernous and tiny rooms, rooms deep in dust or clean as a newt, rooms misshapen or round or precisely square, rooms that themselves contained other rooms, as if they were alive and had children. The place reminded Olivier of an Advent calendar — throw open any door and you'd be guaranteed to find a surprise within.

In fact, Olivier himself was behind just such a door. If you were to put your eye to this keyhole, you'd see him in his room sitting propped up in bed, thinking. Now, most heroes, what with dashing here and there, don't seem to have much time for this, but Olivier considered considering an important prerequisite for any adventure worth its salt. And he knew that an adventure was afoot, for such knowledge was in the very air of this very strange house.

Olivier's thoughts revolved mainly around Gramps, who had only recently married a … witch. Not a real witch, Olivier supposed (that *would* be interesting), but that's what his parents had called Sylvia de Whosit of Whatsit when they'd learned of the match. They said so in capitals — OH NO! NOT THAT WITCH! — making no secret of their feelings. Sylvia was Gramps' third wife, so Olivier called her his step-step-stepgramma. This kept her nicely at a distance. Also, he found himself backing up a step, then another, and another, when he spoke to her.

"Goodness! You make me sound like a dance, step-one-two, step-one-two," she said, whirling around the room in the arms of an invisible partner, cackling.

When the invitation to spend his summer holidays at Cat's Eye Corner had first arrived, his parents had been dead set against it. "But it's not as if she's going to *eat* me," he argued. That is, he hoped not. "Look, I'll keep an *eye* on Gramps and he'll keep an *eye* on me." *What a perfect opportunity for a bit of spying*, thought Olivier. And who better for the job? He was, after all, discreet, stealthy as a shadow, sharp as a tack.

"No way!" his parents chorused, their faces hardened like months-old, lost-under-the-couch Plasticine. But in the end Olivier brought them around. In his skilful hands, their attitude soon warmed and softened and before you could say *prestidigitation* they were smiling and saying, "Well-l-l … all right. But you must promise to call us if there's even a *hint* of trouble. Anything, *any*thing suspicious and we'll be there in a flash."

"Sure thing." His bags were already packed.

Suspicious? There wasn't anything that had happened so far that *wasn't* suspicious.

"*This* place? Are you sure, kid?" asked the taxi driver when he had screeched to a halt in front of the imposing mansion with its turrets and widow's walk. "Tell you what, I'll give you a ride back to the station. No charge."

"Thanks," said Olivier. The house *was* somewhat alarming. "But there's something I have to do here, top secret actually. Can't go into details, you understand. Oh, and may I have a receipt, please?" Best to keep track of business expenses.

"*Dear*, how extraordinarily delightful!" exclaimed Sylvia, greeting him at the door. She gave his arm a little pinch, as though testing it for freshness. "And what a handsome young lad you are. I'll go fetch your grandfather." She drew an ornate silver key out of her pocket and swept off down the dark hall, leaving Olivier to make small talk with a stuffed duck, a hat rack and a huge flat-faced, green-eyed tabby cat with white spats of fur on its feet. It stared at him so intently that he felt he was being sized up for some underling's position in the household.

"Hi," Olivier said, which is about as small as talk can get.

When Gramps appeared, striding a few paces ahead of his formidable bride, Olivier was surprised at how hale he looked, fit and cheery. One of the things he loved about his gramps was how he could always find a flicker of mischief in his face, usually in his eyes or around the corners of his mouth. Olivier was relieved to see it still there, unquenched. Where did she keep him, though, that she needed a key? Gramps threw open his arms and he stepped into them for a close-to-the-heart, peppermint-pocket hug, the soft flannel of his shirt buffing Olivier's cheeks.

"Sylvia, look who's come for dinner!"

"Yes, a *nice* boy."

He hoped she meant guest and *not* main course. Still, Olivier didn't like the way she had said it. He'd better keep on his toes, or somebody might actually end up chewing on them. And what *was* for dinner, anyway?

"Baked mammal," said his step-step-stepgramma.

When he sat down to the table a few minutes later he recalled the cat he'd met at the door and stared hard at the blackish mound heaped on his plate.

"Not hungry?" Gramps asked. "Ah, but you've had a long trip. Why don't I show you up to your room? Get a little shut-eye, eh?"

Gramps really did use expressions like "shut-eye," "by cracky" and "goldarn," as if he'd been to grandfather school and had learned the lingo.

"You know, Ollie," Gramps said, leading him up a steep flight of stairs past walls covered with pictures and maps and shelves crammed with oddments, bottles and books, "this is the goldarnedest, by crackiest house I've ever lived in."

Up and up they climbed. "See that ceiling? Pure

walnut. There are rooms in this place even *I* haven't been in yet. Turn left at the landing, green door. That one's your room. You'll like it, it's got great dust."

"Dust?" Olivier asked, yawning.

"G'night, sleep tight."

"'Night, Gramps."

"Don't let the woodwose bite."

"The *what*?"

"Heh, never mind. See you in the morning."

Dusty didn't *begin* to describe the state of his room — the stuff lay furry and pelt-thick over everything. You could write in it, brand it with your initials, sink your name into it so deeply you would never find it again. *By cracky,* thought Olivier, *they could have cleaned up a bit, at least sheared off the first few coats.* He threw back the covers and jumped into bed fully clothed, teeth unbrushed — this place might not be so bad after all. The flower-patterned sheets were cold as lake water and as he dove into them he imagined himself pushing through petals floppy as lily pads ... deeper and deeper into the mysterious darkness below. If the woodwose did bite that night, he didn't feel a thing.

The next morning, the wondering and worrying part of his thinking done, Olivier decided that what he needed was more material to work with, more evidence. Something was fishy here all right, *something* was going on, but trying to figure out *what* was like trying to knit a pair of socks with only two strands of wool. (Olivier *could* knit, by the way, which is more than you can say for your average, garden-variety hero.) Evidently it was time to do some snooping, time to slip on his sneakers… Oh, yeah, they were already on. What would his mother say? She'd say, "OLIVIER, YOU SLEPT IN YOUR SHOES?" And he'd reply, "Yes, indeed, Mother and see all the time I've saved?"

He smiled to himself as he tiptoed to the door, avoiding telltale *creaks* and *squeaks*. These old floor-boards were mined with alarms and he didn't want his step-step-stepgramma to know he was up yet. He might catch her in the act, doing whatever devious thing it was that he suspected she did. At the door, he crouched down, peered through the keyhole to check if the coast was clear and … who was *that?* Someone was staring brazenly back at him. He immediately threw open the door, prepared to confront whoever it was, and — nothing! No one was there. He ran into the hall, searching up and down, but whoever it was had completely vanished.

Excellent. He rolled up his sleeves and rubbed his hands together. Far from being frightened or alarmed, Olivier felt invigorated. No point in calling his parents now, because what might have been suspicious had taken a step beyond that into the inexplicable. His folks had always advised him to keep an open mind, but surely they didn't mean *this* open.

He strode off down the hall, noting that every single door was closed tight. Odder still was the fact that each door was different in size, shape and colour: portals with personality. One was tall and narrow, painted a priestly black, with a plain worn doorknob. Another was wide and square as a judge, made of thick polished oak and fitted with a chunky brass handle. Here was an elegant door made of pine, decked out with a cut-glass knob and a fanlight hovering like a halo on top. Next to it was an infant-size door, stained red as a berry, with a tiny silver knob.

Olivier knew he probably shouldn't, but he decided to try a few. Can't be a perfect guest *and* a spy. Besides, what if Gramps was behind one of them, tongue-tied, labouring captive under some witchy spell? Olivier approached a dreary-looking grey door that had chipped paint and a marble knob that was eerily cold to the touch. He gave it a good twist. Locked. Somehow this didn't surprise him, and in the case of this depressing customer, didn't bother him much either. All right, next. Also locked. He began moving from door to door, testing every one as if shaking hands in a reception line at a wedding. They were *all* locked.

He reached down to try the last door, the little one, pinching its tiny knob between thumb and forefinger as if it were a dial on a radio. It turned and swung open with a thin, creaking whine. Instantly, Olivier flattened himself on the floor and looked through. He expected to see a storage space, a nook or a boot closet. Instead, a room of regular proportions stretched out before him, and, from what he could see, it looked quite cozy and inviting. Big comfy chairs were arranged around an open hearth in which a fire gently burned, flames licking quietly at a couple of logs placed on two figured andirons. (These were also called "firedogs." He knew this because his mother collected them.) The room was a mess, but a happy one, with stacks of books piled here and there, games spread out on the floor, sheet music cascading off a stand. A grand piano filled one corner — a pogo stick propped against it — and glass cases containing fossils and insects took up another. In the centre of the room lay a deep red, intricately patterned Persian carpet. It was the kind you could easily imagine having a magic thread woven into it, the kind that just might take you places.

Indeed, although this room was not *that* unusual, it gave Olivier a most curious feeling. Not only because he had discovered it behind an improbably small door, but also because if he were to dream up a room in which to settle contentedly on a long rainy afternoon, this would be it. Furthermore, there were provisions: a half-moon mahogany table positively groaned with heaped plates of sandwiches, iced cupcakes and a fat pot of tea, a wispy beckoning finger of steam curling out of the spout. And he hadn't eaten breakfast yet, let alone dinner last night.

The room also contained dozens of cats (not exaggerating one hair). The place was practically decorated with them — cats of every stripe and spot, swag-bellied or lean, curled or crouched, lolling and sprawling, washing their faces, scratching their fleas or simply doing what cats do best — staring. And at the moment most were staring at *him*.

Someone distinctly said, "*Olivier*, at last, you've made it. We've been waiting ever so long. Why don't you *step step step* right in. It's time you met the Poets."

TWO

Naturally it was his step-step-stepgramma who had spoken and now she said something else, which sounded like, "mumble mumble mirror." A spell of some sort?

"I beg your pardon?" asked Olivier, as he squeezed himself through the snug doorway, wriggling and pulling himself forward.

"In the keyhole, my dear, it was a *mirror*. Didn't you guess?" She gazed down at him, greatly amused, as he finally squirmed through and got to his feet. He hadn't seen her in the room at first, as she'd been perusing a bookshelf in the corner, hidden from view. Frankly, he wasn't too thrilled to see her at all, for he would have liked nothing better than to be left alone to check out the games and the collections in the glass cases and maybe try out the pogo stick or plonk out a tune on the piano or leaf through some of the books.

"A mirror? What for?" he asked.

"Why, a little self-reflection never hurt anyone, now did it? Especially for a private eye," she smiled. "Isn't that droll?"

Might be, but the eye he'd seen was blue. His own were brown.

" 'Droll.' I'd let you look it up, but I can't seem to find my dictionary. Anyway, it means 'humorous.'"

"Yes, I *know*," he said. At least, he did now.

"Would you like to jump on the furniture?" She gestured toward the chubby and enormously comfy-looking chairs.

"That would be nice," he said, wondering what she had up her sleeve. When adults start inviting you to jump on the furniture, beware.

"Go ahead, then. Feel free."

"It's not half so much fun when you're allowed."

"Clever child. Let's eat. Cozy up to the fire there and I'll bring you some sandwiches. Tell me, would you like 16 or 17?"

"One or two will do nicely, thanks." He couldn't fault her for her hospitality, even if the food was poisoned.

"My, you can't be very hungry. Might as well move on to dessert." He had no problem with that, really, and while she piled cupcakes on to a plate with a pair of silver tongs, he sat down in a chair close to the fire-place, sinking comfortably into its mossy green bulk.

"Cup of tea or a glass of wine?"

"Tea, please." He *was* on duty, after all.

Once she had provided him with a brimming cup of sweet milky tea and a mound of cupcakes, which he began to demolish, Sylvia seated herself in the chair opposite and said, "Isn't there something you'd like to ask me?"

"Mmmhmph." The cupcakes had a muffling effect, but he still managed to say, "Poets. You said I was to meet some. Where are they?" He had expected some weird friends of hers with beards, wild hair and dirty fingernails.

"My dear, you are surrounded by them."

"You mean the *cats*?" The creatures had kept so strangely still since he'd come into the room, he had begun to wonder if they were stuffed.

"They're much more sedate than they used to be," Sylvia sighed. "Take themselves far too seriously, you know. They used to be 'pets,' plain and simple, but then some Inklings stuck a letter 'o' in when I wasn't paying attention and now, you see, they're all 'poets.' That's Gertrude, the tubby calico over by the potted palm, Emily's hiding behind it. There's Delmore on the carpet beside Dylan — both scamps, been into the catnip, I'm afraid. They're quite sozzled. Anonymous is the white longhair washing her face. Eliot's the grey dignified one holding court on the arm of the sofa. Those black kittens asleep in the basket are Edgar, Allan and Poe. And Bliss here I believe you've already met. *Not* at dinner, I might add."

True enough. The big tabby cat that was tucked

into a round furry ball beside her chair was the same animal he had encountered yesterday at the front door. The cat had been snoozing, but lightly, for the moment Olivier turned his attention to him Bliss raised his great head and gave him a look that suggested he knew something that Olivier assuredly did not.

"Did you say, um, Inklings?" It occurred to him then that she might simply be a bit batty. Cuckoo, cracked as a plate, scrambled as an egg. That would explain a lot, actually.

"I did."

Neither said anything further for a moment, then Sylvia added, "Better be careful, Olivier, or they'll have no end of sport with your name."

"How?" Best to humour her.

"Why, they could sneak up on it in the middle of the night when it's fast asleep, steal a couple of its letters and when you woke up in the morning you'd be plain old Liver. I shouldn't like to be called Liver for the rest of my days."

Olivier laughed. "My name doesn't sleep. It doesn't *do* anything. It's just a name."

"My dear, never underestimate your name. You might be surprised what it can do for you."

"Wait a minute. I don't even know what these things are. I thought an Inkling was a kind of idea, a hunch. Nothing real or alive."

"They *are* difficult to spot. They're thin as hints and travel in undertones. They love notions and rumours, as well as old books, paper, binding and bookmarks.

Gracious, you know how bookmarks always seem to go missing? You set one down, read for a bit, reach for it to mark your place and … it's gone. Some Inkling's made off with it."

Instead of getting all snotty and uppity about this explanation and saying, "What nonsense!" or "How unscientific!" he said, "I'd love to see one."

"Do you think at all?"

"Every morning, first thing. Mental callisthenics, my father calls it."

"Yes, well, then I expect you'll see one before long. Musing seems to attract them like bees to nectar."

"They don't always steal things, do they? You did say they *added* a letter to 'pets'."

"They're tinkerers — word renovators and improvisers. But not all of their changes are for the better. Mind you, anyone can have pets; it's much more interesting to have poets lolling about the house. What I'm concerned about is your list, Olivier. What might they do to *that*? Why, you'll be searching for all the wrong things."

He must have been getting the hang of chatting with her, for he knew that if he sat perfectly still, in two flicks of a cat's tail she'd tell him what she was going on about. And she did.

"I am referring of course to the scavenger hunt, a game that promises to be the most difficult, puzzling, hilarious and dangerous ever devised by an exceptionally talented and refined host, me, for the entertainment and delight of a charming young guest, you."

"I like scavenger hunts. I had one at my last birthday party. We had to look for a pebble, a piece of glass, a bottle cap, a dandelion, a burr and a feather. It was great! Everyone thought so, until Horace Speechly fell and cut his hand on the glass. But then, he hurts himself at my party every year. It's a tradition of sorts. He always gets Band-Aids in his treat bag."

"What a clumsy, witless child. I'm afraid your list would do him in. It would be *far far far* too challenging."

"Sounds good." And very crafty of her. "Where is it? When do I start?"

"Your grandfather has it."

"Ah."

"In a way, he is the first item, if you will, on the last. I mean, list. You must fund him to fond out what you need to fend. Drat, those pesky Inklings! *Find*, Olivier, *find, find.*"

THREE

After crawling back through the tiny doorway into the hall, it took Olivier exactly 52.5 seconds to find his gramps. This was on account of Gramps *not* being hidden under the floorboards, rolled up in a rug or stuffed in a grandfather clock, but clearly visible to anyone glancing out of an upstairs window and down into the garden below, which Olivier happened to do in passing. *Some scavenger hunt*, he thought, as he caught sight of Gramps moving among the greenery wielding a huge pair of shears. *Puzzling, eh? Difficult, huh?* Olivier bet he'd find everything on that list before the morning was out.

In another 52.5 seconds, he was standing beside his gramps watching him *snip snip snip* at a shrub. Not that you could call what he was snipping at a shrub exactly. It was more like a shaggy green *person*

— a cross between a man and a bush — and Gramps was grooming him by snipping off stray twigs and leaves.

"Like 'im?"

"I sure do, Gramps. Is this your hobby?"

"This is my job. Sylvia doesn't like this fella to get too scruffy."

Olivier studied the shrub man more closely. He was expertly shaped, with well-defined features and hands that looked almost real. With a puff of wind he might just come to life and dash away.

"A work of art," Olivier concluded.

"Yep."

As Gramps didn't add anything further, he decided it was time to ask about the list.

Gramps dropped the shears and started slapping the sides of his pants and jacket. "I had it right here." He then proceeded to draw from any number of pockets a variety of objects. "Hold this a sec, will you?" and he piled into Olivier's hands a deck of cards, a screwdriver, a pair of castanets, a piece of toast, a magnifying glass, an elastic band, a fork, a paintbrush, a dried worm, an arrowhead, a cork with a coin stuck in the top, a pink sponge, a sock and a Brussels sprout. It struck Olivier that he'd found everything that might be on a scavenger hunt list, except the list.

"Wait a minute, wait a minute," said Gramps, retrieving the objects from Olivier in the same order he'd handed them to him and putting them all back in the very same pockets. "I set it down when I was in the parlour. That's it. I set it down because I was looking for a ... a ... heck, *what* was I looking for?" As if to jog his memory, he picked up the shears again and began snipping absent-mindedly at the bush, unfortunately slicing off two of the green man's fingers, as well as the wayward sprouting tip of his nose. "Oops," he said. Then, reassuringly, "Not to worry, it'll grow back." He turned to Olivier and said, "I expect you'll find it before long."

"But I don't even know where to look."

"You will, you will."

Olivier ran back to the house, thinking that this game might not be such a piece of cake after all. In order to find one thing, it seemed you had to find another first. Before he could even start to search for anything on the list, he had to find the list, which was in the parlour, wherever *that* was.

Fortunately, he liked to read, so he had encountered the odd parlour or two in the pages of old books. As rooms go, he got the impression that parlours were usually stiff and formal, full of uncomfortable horsehair furniture, highly waxed tables, fussy knickknacks and doilies. Parlours were where you received your guests and, assuming that his step-step-stepgramma had any of those, her parlour would likely be located near the front door.

Wrong. An hour later he was still poking around, wandering up and down corridors, sticking his head into closets and storerooms. He had discovered a conservatory, a laboratory, a library, two kitchens, a sewing room full of peculiar costumes (which he would have examined more closely if he weren't on a mission) and, honestly, many other rooms to which he couldn't even put a name. But no parlour. And Gramps was right. This *was* the goldarnedest, by crackiest house. He was positive that he had peeked into some of the same rooms twice and the second time they had changed somehow; they *looked* different.

Exasperated, but determined, Olivier decided to start at the front door — if he could find it — and try again. He retraced his steps along the first floor hallway until he was back at the entrance. He turned, walked a few paces and opened the first door on his left. As he did, he heard a rustling sound coming from within, followed by an urgent whispering and then a clattering noise. He slipped inside. The room was dim, its window shades drawn tightly against the light. Olivier stood perfectly still, but could see no one. He moved farther into the room, thinking this must be where Sylvia kept her fancier furnishings — porcelain figurines, a satiny chesterfield, doily-scabbed tables and chairs. *This* was that rogue parlour he'd been looking for. "How could I have missed it?" he asked aloud, half hoping that someone would answer. It was obvious, however, that he was alone.

Something caught his eye. A glittering object lay at the base of a spindle-legged glass table in the corner. *Oho*, he thought. It was a dagger, small, delicate and exquisitely fashioned, with a silver blade and a gold embossed hilt. He picked it up and lay it across his palm. The scale of it made him think of a toy, but a wicked one, sharp and cool. What was it for? Trimming the hedges?

Olivier snatched a doily off the arm of a chair (she wouldn't miss one, he reasoned, they seemed to spread like fungus) and carefully wrapped the dagger. He slipped the lacy bundle into his pocket, where it lodged among some marbles (two oilies and a toothpaste) a string ball and a package of gum. His pocketful of stuff didn't rival that of his gramps, but at least it was the start of a basic collection. *Now*, he thought, scouting around on the floor, checking under chairs, lifting cushions, *where's that list?*

Something ghostly white drifted down off the mantel and past his shoulder. Olivier spun around and plucked it out of the air — a sheet of filmy onionskin paper. He stared hard at the mantel for a moment, but couldn't see anything, not even a scurrying mouse that might have dislodged it. Turning his attention to what he assumed was the list, he saw that it wasn't that at all, but a message of some sort that had come unravelled:

in   a   b
loo   y o   h   d   r
   k   Ur   e   o a

You'd almost think the words were floating, as if someone had given the paper a vigorous shake or blown forcefully upon it.

Olivier liked word games, so he found that most of this odd message fell into place readily enough. "Look in yo Ur," he read. Aha, "your." Look in your ... "head"? What? He had to make the list up himself? Okay, so. What does a "b-o-a-r" have to do with anything? He thought of wild boar, Obelix's favourite food in the Asterix books, but he didn't suppose that was relevant. "Head boar?" In your head ... boar ... d. Right, that's it, the letter "d" is missing, probably tumbled right off the page. Or stolen.

Not being one to stand around twiddling his thumbs when there was work to be done, Olivier tore out of the room and ran up the stairs, taking them two and three at a time, while a niggling thought trailed in the air behind him. *Was it really, could it have been ... his first encounter with ... Inklings?*

FOUR

Olivier burst through the door of his room in exactly the way one should for a story to unfold with a certain amount of dash. (He'd tried this a few times at home and no one much appreciated it). Although intent on finding the list, he couldn't help but notice that, like the oddly changeable rooms downstairs, his room looked *different*. It was clean for one thing, magnificently so. Every last speck of dust was gone, as if the whole mass had gathered itself up like a shaggy beast and stomped off to some other room. Who might have done this? Not Sylvia, that's for sure.

He jumped on his bed to check out the headboard. It was the kind with a cabinet built into it, more like a bookcase, with a sliding panel at each end. It was the perfect place to stash letters, comics, drawings, private papers and, possibly, very likely, a scavenger hunt list.

He slid back the left-hand panel and … *nothing* … except for a ratty old fountain pen that someone had obviously pitched into this side of the headboard and forgotten.

"Cheap," said Olivier, picking it up and examining it. "Probably doesn't work." He tossed it onto the bed and slid back the other panel. And *there* it was! A parchment scroll tied with a ribbon red as a tongue. Thrilled, he seized the scroll, untied the ribbon and unrolled it. He held it open before him, like a messenger with a royal proclamation, and read:

hagoday
armlet
blood
skipjack
web
sunstone
brain coral
doit

Olivier groaned and fell back on the bed, letting the scroll roll itself up with a *snap* like a window shade. "Hagoday"? "Sunstone"? "Doit"? What on earth was a "doit"? Some of these things had more than *one* meaning. A "skipjack" was a kind of fish, but also a kind of beetle. Which one was he supposed to find? If the word had two meanings, why not 10? A couple of the items on the list weren't too specific, like "blood" (*ew*, that was a weird one) and "web." At least he knew what an "armlet" was, although getting his hands on one would be a challenge. What he needed was a dictionary. Surely there would be one in that library downstairs, if it hadn't turned into some other room by now and if he could find it again. He decided to write a question mark beside the objects on the list that he didn't know. He picked up the fountain pen and gave it a good shake before unscrewing the lid. Dry as a bone was what he expected as he unrolled the scroll and positioned the pen beside the first item on the list. Not so.

!% ^ $#(*Æ + }!!

The pen seemed to be writing on its own. It then wrote, *Cheap? Cheap is it?* This was followed by more typographical expletives, followed by, *I'll have you know that I'm a blue blood, related to the Parkers on one side and the Mont Blancs on the other. Hmph!*

What is going on? thought Olivier, unable to resist allowing it to continue. *Don't squeeze me so tight, you wretched boy, I can hardly breathe. And don't try shaking me again, either, or I'll spit indelible ink on your fingers.*

Olivier instantly dropped the pen and stared at it in alarm.

"Are you *alive*?" he asked. The pen had grown extremely warm in his hand, but then it *was* overwrought. (Overwrit, in this case.) It answered as best it could by shooting a contemptuous stream of black ink across the bed covers.

"I don't expect Sylvia will like that," said Olivier, astonished. An articulate writing instrument? Well, he'd already been rude enough and didn't want to make things worse by refusing to believe in it.

"I *am* sorry," he apologized, jumping off the bed to fetch a small notebook from his suitcase. He'd brought it with him to record his observations about Cat's Eye Corner and Sylvia de Whosit of Whatsit, but now saw that it might be useful to hold a conversation. "I've never met one of your kind before. I didn't mean to treat you like … an object."

He climbed back onto the bed, flipped open the notebook and picked up the pen very carefully and respectfully.

Right, the pen wrote. *Murray here. What's your name?*

"Olivier."

Olivier, hmm. How posh. Named after the actor?

"Great uncle. I like Murray awfully well. It suits you. It's a strong name."

The pen seemed to glow at this. *How old are you?*

"Eleven. And you?"

Eighty-three.

"That's pretty old."

I'm vastly experienced. What do you do for a living?

"I have a paper route and I collect pop bottles. I get an allowance, so I'm paid for being a kid. Right now I'm a spy, strictly freelance. What do you do?"

I am a writer, naturally.

"No kidding. Published?"

Murray's ink, a lovely peacock blue, began to darken ominously at this query, so Olivier quickly veered off in another conversational direction. "Say, since you're a writer and must know words inside out, maybe you could help me with this scavenger hunt list."

Thought you'd never ask. Let's proceed in an orderly fashion, my boy. What's first?

"'Hagoday.' Do you know what that is?"

Knock, knock.

"Um, who's there?"

What?

"What, who?"

What, what?

"What, what, who?"

Good gravy, lad. Speak a language we both understand, will you?

"You mean to tell me you've been around for 83 years and you don't know what a knock knock joke is?"

You said you were a spy. I was giving you a clue. "Knock, knock"? "Hagoday"? You know, a door knocker?

"Really?"

Yes, they are also called "sanctuary knockers." You'll find them on churches, old buildings. Highly decorative — lions' heads, monsters, that sort of thing. It's said that if someone is chasing you and you reach the hagoday and lay hold of it, you'll be safe. Your pursuer will be powerless to touch you.

"Home free. Where would I find one of those?"

Europe would be your best bet.

"I can hardly go there. No, I think it has to be around here somewhere, or my step-step-stepgramma wouldn't have put it on the list. She's strange, maybe even a witch, but I've got a feeling she's still fair. There are lots of doors here, one of them probably has this knocker on it. Why don't we look?"

I am rather thirsty, you know. It's been ages since I've had a dram. Let's rustle up a beverage first, say, some Chinese calligraphic, or a spot of Indian black?

"Hey, Murray, you know what, you could be my new *pen* pal."

Ha, ha! His laugh was so appreciative it took up most of the page. *So I could, my boy, so I could.*

FIVE

Branches scraped against the window in what Olivier guessed was the absolute middle of the night. His room was as black as the blackest ink. He touched the breast pocket of his shirt where Murray lay dreaming in syllables. They'd had a marvellous day, Olivier running up and down stairs, in and out of rooms, Murray in one hand, their notebook in the other. They had plenty to talk about, too, for they came across the most curious objects. One room, which had contained a display of antique weaponry, crossbows and samurai swords, also had a large globe stuck in a dusty corner. It revealed whole countries, lakes and cities of which Olivier had never even *heard*.

In another room, lined up on an otherwise bare shelf, they had found a pair of bone china fangs, a moustache cup, red plastic lips, a glass eye, a false nose (size XL) and a family pack of hairy stick-on moles. It was an odd and slightly unsettling assembly, but neither of them had known quite what to say about it, so they had moved to the centre of the room where a game board was set up on a card table. Three chairs were positioned around the table, as though all was ready for a trio of friends to sit down and begin playing. The game wasn't one with which Olivier was familiar, but it looked intriguing. The board depicted a dense forest, a number of trails running through it, as well as a winding river. A few tree-houses peeked out of the foliage, a vine-covered cottage sat in a clearing, a marshy area held a small hut, a carnival of some sort was positioned near one edge of the board and a tower fronting a very dark lake stood near the other. While he studied these various features Olivier had *thought* he'd seen a quiver of movement in the forest, as if a slight breeze had passed through it. And on the surface of that dark and chilly-looking lake, there had been a shimmer of motion — a cat's paw racing lightly over the surface.

"Did you see that?" he had asked.

Murray, who had been busily doodling away to himself (with Olivier's help, of course), had penned the word "topiary." The funny thing about this word, outside of having nothing to do with anything, was how it had almost instantly disappeared off the paper, starting with the tail of the "y" and winking out at the tip of the "t." It unwrote itself.

"Hey, what happened?" Olivier had asked.

Murray had responded with, *Oh nothing, just inking*

out loud. Did you take note of that game piece there?

Olivier had lifted a game piece off the board, the only one on it in fact, and examined it closely. It was a tiny but exact replica of the shrub man that Gramps had been trimming in the garden. How strange! But stranger still, and this had made him catch his breath, two of the man's minuscule fingers were shorter than the others and the end of his nose was blunt, as though recently nipped off.

Surprising, indeed. He couldn't help but think of it now as he lay in bed, fully awake, listening to the branches scratching against the window, scratching at his very brain. Why *was* that game piece so like the topiary shrub, which, as Murray explained, was what you called such ornamental tree art? He regretted not having looked inside the carved wooden box that sat to one side of the game, for it must have contained the rest of the game pieces. Now, he wondered what they would have looked like.

Olivier wished he could sleep as easily as Murray. Then, in the pitch black room, with the wind blustering outside pushing the tree branches against the glass, a thought came to him that made him sit straight up in bed. *There are no large trees outside this bedroom. There aren't any on this side of the house at all.* He jumped out of bed and groped his way to the window, yanked the heavy curtain aside and found himself staring into a tangled mass of swaying branches just beyond the glass. They were barely illuminated by a silver trickle of moonlight. Before bed, Olivier had stood at this very spot gazing at fields and a distant forest. He had even imagined exploring them with Murray once the scavenger hunt was over.

Another sound seemed to be coming from outside his bedroom door. *Scritch, scritch.* There it was again. It sounded very much like some sort of clawed creature trying to get in. Olivier immediately thought of rats, which he understood to be charming and intelligent animals. Still, he'd rather make the acquaintance of one during the more sociable daylight hours.

He considered jumping back into bed and hiding under the covers until the noise went away. Instead, he crept quietly to the door and slowly, very slowly, opened it a crack, an eye-width, just enough to peek out. There stood Bliss, the tabby cat, looking highly inconvenienced and twitching his tail with impatience. As soon as he saw Olivier, he turned and padded off down the hall, glancing back at him once as if to say, "What are you waiting for? Come on."

Olivier didn't need to be asked twice. Actually, he would like to have been asked once. Considering what had happened so far — his discovery of Murray, the flicker of animation in the game board, the sudden appearance of trees at his window — you wouldn't think that a talking cat would be stretching things much. Other children in other adventures got to talk to animals he reasoned, as he hurried up the hall after Bliss. It was only fair that he should, too. Bliss, however, said absolutely nothing and, moving with a shadowy feline stealth, disappeared through an open doorway at the end of the hall.

Olivier followed eagerly, as this was one of the doors — arched at the top like a castle or cathedral door and made of rough plain wood — that had been locked earlier in the day. He slipped in and instantly a gust of wind hit him full in the face. But there were no windows in the room, only thick, pitted stone walls poorly lit by candles flickering in sconces. It was as bare as a cell, not a stick of furniture in it. The room felt cold and damp and smelled slightly musty. He wondered if he should wake up Murray and let him know what was going on (whatever *was* going on), but he didn't want to lose track of Bliss, who had headed straight into the shadows at the other end of the room. The shadows deepened, growing darker and darker; the room seemed endless. Bliss was nowhere in sight. Olivier himself was nowhere in sight — he couldn't even see his hands any more!

"Bliss!" he called out. "What's going on? Where are you?"

No answer. If the cat could speak, now would be a darn good time to hear from him. But he didn't.

Olivier reached out, moving sideways until he touched the wall with one hand, then, continuing forward, he became aware that the wall's texture was changing. Stone gave way to a smoother material that felt like plaster, which then turned into something papery, like birch bark. Then, *ugh*, he pulled his hand back in alarm. The wall had begun to feel warm as skin and muscled, like the flank of a horse. This action must have woken Murray, for Olivier sensed his suddenly agitated presence in his shirtfront pocket. Too bad he wasn't a penlight. Olivier quickly explained the situation and cast his vote for pressing on. Getting the impression that Murray agreed, Olivier once again reached out for the wall.

The wall grew fur as he continued to move ahead. It got shaggier and shaggier and occasionally his fingers caught in tangles and matted hair. (Imagine grooming the walls of your house!) The room also began to slope downward and he soon encountered steps that were very awkward to walk on for they were both unevenly spaced and rounded. He bent down to run his hand along their surface and concluded they were, indeed, what he suspected — stairs made of tree roots. The room began to lighten and the air smelled sweeter, earthier, reminding him of hyacinths and lily-of-the-valley and freshly dug gardens. Now large gaps appeared in the wall through which he could stick his hand. The house, as if undecided as to *what* it wanted to be, had straggled to a stop like a fey unfinished sentence.

Finally, more out than in, Olivier surveyed the scene, a faint wash of moonlight allowing him to get his bearings. He had not, as yet, spent much time outside Cat's Eye Corner, but he knew it when he saw it — the hedges, the garden, the barn, the fields beyond — and this definitely wasn't it. For one thing, the house, which now looked very old and decrepit, was almost completely surrounded by an ancient forest, its oaks, beeches and elms gnarled and knobbly with age. A wind rushing through the topmost branches gave Olivier the feeling that he was standing in the heart of a deep green ocean. A shudder of apprehension ran up his spine.

As for Bliss, he was sitting about 10 feet away, licking one white paw that he held curled in front of his face like a furry ice cream cone.

"There you are!" Olivier said, reaching into his shirt-front pocket for Murray. He got out the notebook and Murray wrote, *Wait*.

"*Huh?*"

Wait! Murray repeated, in louder, **bolder** writing.

Did he mean he wanted Bliss to wait? Olivier glanced sharply at the cat and said, "Be a good kitty, OK? Don't run off without us." But Bliss certainly did not wait. He cast them a scornful look, one of those maddeningly unreadable cat stares, then he turned and dove into the engulfing darkness.

SIX

"Let's go!"

Wait.

"You said that already, Murray. We *can't* wait or we'll lose sight of Bliss altogether."

For a spy you're not very observant, you know.

"What do you mean?"

Notice anything unusual about that stand of trees over there?

Eyes. Pairs of them, constellations of them, bright and sharp, shone from the branches of the weathered remains of an orchard.

"What are they?" he whispered.

Don't be alarmed, my boy. It's only the Poets. No one's afraid of poets.

After walking over to the trees, Olivier could see the cats more clearly, sitting upright or draped languidly

over branches. He even recognized the kittens —
Edgar, Allan and Poe — peeking out of a hollow in a
tree trunk, filling it like darkness itself. They all seemed
to be watching him very, very closely.

"Meeeeeowwwww," one of them said suddenly. This
was only for openers, a brief introductory statement
before going on at some length, mewing, meowing,
yowling and even growling.

Hmm, yes, scribbled Murray.

"Mrew, mrew," another cat said, pointedly.

I see. That is a problem.

"Murray, do you understand what they're saying?"

*Well, I do know some Catonese, yes. Just a whisker,
un petit mew, you might say.*

"But that's great. Excellent. So, what are they talking
about? What do we have to do next? Any hints to help
us find the things on the list?"

*No, actually they were arguing the merits of leonine
rhyme over blank verse.*

"Poetry?"

You're surprised?

"Sort of."

You thought they'd be talking about us?

"It *is* our adventure."

*Ah, but these are cats, Olivier, cats. "C-a-t-s" spells
unpredictable and unknowable. Why don't you ask them
for advice? You never know, they might be in the mood to
cooperate. Go ahead, I'll translate.*

"All right." Olivier squared his shoulders and
stepped several paces nearer the trees. "Mr. Eliot, sir,"

he began, uncertain if this was the correct form of address, but figuring the courtesy would not go amiss, "would you happen to have any idea what we should do next?"

Eliot was the colour of a business suit, a slate grey tom with a great round head and green eyes. The cat blinked once, slowly, before answering with a couple of clipped, succinct meows.

"Well?" said Olivier.

Murray wrote not a word. As it was so unlike him to be short of them, Olivier wondered if he had gone dry.

Hah, guess what? He said we should have followed Bliss. We've missed our chance.

"Never mind, Murray." Olivier was surprised at how flushed and red his friend's ink now appeared and he sympathized. "It doesn't matter in the least. We'll work it out for ourselves."

But then another cat spoke up, quietly but insistently. It was the calico named Gertrude.

"Ach, mew," said yet another, a brindled kitty with ears that folded over like the dog-eared pages of a book.

Olivier pricked up his own ears. The brindled kitty actually seemed to smile at him and Eliot nodded his head thoughtfully. He then addressed Olivier and Murray again, only this time in a more purringly pleasant tone.

Ho ho, remarked Murray. *It looks like they have a favour to ask of us. Our bargaining position has just improved considerably.*

"Really? What do they want?"

It seems that they are having some trouble with the Inklings.

"So Inklings *do* exist?"

Oh, certainly. But they're hard to pin down and apparently they've become more active lately, making a real nuisance of themselves, stealing letters, switching them around, scrambling words, whole poems even. Terrible. Like having verbal termites.

"How can we help, though?"

Find out what's going on. They think there must be somebody else behind it, someone stirring them up, making them restless, giving them ideas. Hah, that's rich, Inklings with ideas.

"A mastermind," Olivier said, thrilled. "I wonder who?"

Exactly. No one knows. Eliot thinks it might be quite serious. He says we should call on a fellow named Sylvan Blink who lives somewhere in the Drak Woulds. He might be able to give us some information.

"The 'Drak Woulds,' Murray?"

Several of the Poets began to yowl, sending up a great caterwaul of complaint.

You see! You see what's happened? Used to be "Dark Woods" and now what do we have? The "Drak Woulds". Tsk, tsk. I can understand why they're upset. Think what the little busybodies might do to Dickens, to Shakespeare. "Oh that this too too solid fish would melt". Imagine!

"But aren't the 'Poets' themselves the result of Inkling tinkering? Otherwise they'd be, you know, 'pets'?"

"Meeoww, ow, owww," replied Eliot, curtly.

Yes, a good point, but he claims that some editing is superior to others. And necessary.

"Mew, mew."

This pint-sized voice belonged to one of the black kittens, which had climbed out of the tree's hollow and was twining around Olivier's legs.

It's Poe. He wants to go with us.

"Mew."

Oops, she wants to go with us, rather.

"How nice." Olivier bent down and lightly scrubbed the top of Poe's head, hoping this wasn't a breach of decorum. She responded by purring even more loudly.

This request did, however, provoke a great deal of cat consternation — and conversation. Some said that she was too young, while others maintained that it would do her good. She was spunky and resourceful and had already explored some of the great Woulds. Besides, as the medical cat, Dr. Faustus, reminded them, Poe needed a break from her gloomy and intro-spective brothers, who did nothing all day but mutter to themselves about ravens.

Bah! wrote Murray, with impatience. *She'll do what she wants, anyway. Now, say "ahem."*

"Ahem?"

With some authority, please.

"Ahem," said Olivier, with some authority.

All cat chat immediately ceased and all eyes again focused on Olivier, as if he were about to make a speech. Fortunately, Eliot picked up the "ahem" where Olivier left off and went on to say something of significance. That's the impression he gave, anyway.

Aha! Let's have a look in the hollow of that tree, my boy.

"OK." Olivier walked over to the old tree and reached into the hollow, which caused Edgar and Allan to scamper out with a hiss of annoyance. The inside of the tree felt powdery with decay and there were rough, jagged bits sticking up — he hoped he wouldn't get a sliver. He searched carefully until the tips of his fingers touched a soft, mossy nest. In the centre of this sat a smooth, roundish object, which he lifted out of the hollow. It didn't really feel like a bird's egg, for the very good reason that it wasn't one — it was a stone, a gem of some sort, yellowish and opalescent, winking at him in the moonlight.

A cat's-eye.

"Right. I've seen pictures of cat's-eyes in books, but this is the first real one I've ever seen. It's beautiful."

Indeed, said Murray, a bit grumpily, as Olivier juggled the gem, the notebook and his pen pal. *And it is of great value to the Poets. They are entrusting it to us, for helping them. Eliot claims that it will come in handy. Oh, and he wishes us luck. He says we'll need it. Not sure I like the sound of that.*

"I guess that means it's time to go. Are you ready, Poe?"

"Mew!" answered the kitten and before Olivier could say anything more, she took off into the forest.

Not again, Murray grumbled.

Olivier cried, "Wait!"

SEVEN

"Mew, mew."

"Sorry, Poe, I can't see what you're saying. I mean, it's too dark in here for Murray to translate. Why don't you just speak English?"

"Mew?"

Olivier sighed and walked on. They were following a meandering path through the forest, soft underfoot with fallen pine needles. Murray was riding in his shirtfront pocket like a tar in a crow's nest, while Poe scampered along beside. She was a shadow that zipped ahead, dashed back, shot up a tree trunk and then scudded back down again, claws scrabbling.

"Don't run too far ahead," he warned, as Poe took off. How were they to know what danger — animal, mineral or otherwise — might lie around the next knurl and twist of the path? The Inklings may have fiddled with the name of the Drak Woulds, but their meddling certainly hadn't shed much light on it. Or in it. He didn't have any idea where they were going and only the vaguest of plans: to find this Sylvan Blink fellow. At least he still had the dagger if they ran into any kind of trouble. Actually, Olivier had forgotten all about it, being so busy with Murray and the scavenger hunt, and had only remembered it when he had slipped the cat's-eye into his pants pocket. He'd give it to Gramps as soon as they got back. Definitely ... whenever that might be. The path wound on and on; they followed it up and down, in and around, until finally they untied it like a knot. After a while light began to filter down through the tops of the trees. Morning had broken.

Amazingly, Poe was still frisking about, a tireless ball of energy. Once again she bounded ahead of them and out of sight. This time, though, she ran right into that trouble Olivier had earlier anticipated. Poe's tiny voice suddenly expanded and she made a sound much larger than herself; "MRREEEOWW!" This was followed by a deep and alarming silence, then by an agonized howling, weeping, sniffling, moaning and somewhat theatrical boo-hooing. Someone, but not Poe, seemed to be sampling every possible variety of unhappiness.

As Olivier raced along the path, he could feel Murray in his shirtfront pocket go cold with fear. They rounded the bend and Olivier skidded to a stop. Poe was nowhere in sight, but before them, propped up against the trunk of a massive spruce, was a largish, greenish man. His face was buried in his huge hands and he was crying, with some gusto and abandon, as the pinecone curls of his hair bobbed vigorously up and down. Patches of lichen grew on his green skin, the odd leaf sprouted here and there and he was dressed in a tunic made of bark, cinched at the waist with a vine of Deadly Nightshade.

He looked harmless enough, especially in his woeful state, so Olivier ventured a question. "Excuse me," he said very softly, "you wouldn't happen to have seen our companion, a little black cat? She passed by here only a second ago?"

"I thought it was licorice," the poor fellow sobbed, his face firmly planted in his hands. "Just a lick, that's all I wanted, a little taste. It *hurt* me."

Oh dear. Wherever Poe was, she had clearly gotten the better of him. "Did she scratch you badly?" Olivier stepped closer and noticed a tiny nick in his hand out of which a trickle of sap seemed to be oozing. Although this wasn't much to be blubbering about, he did notice something else that gave him a start. When Olivier had first spotted him, he'd thought of the topiary shrub and the game piece and now he saw that this green man *also* had two fingers shorter than the others — the ends nicked off!

The sorrowful creature raised his head to reveal his nose, which, sure enough, was docked at the tip. He gazed imploringly at Olivier and said, "You're not angry with me?" He could hardly get the words out.

"Not at all. It wasn't your fault. I don't suppose

you've ever seen a kitten before." Although where he might have encountered four-footed walking licorice was a good question.

Olivier's kindness seemed to cheer up the leafy fellow and a tentative smile began to form on his pleasant green face (the colour of spring leaves). Then, suddenly, he balked, his eyes bulged like boiled eggs and he turned an even deeper shade of green (summer leaves).

"Gosh, what's wrong? Can we help?" Olivier hastily reached for Murray and the notebook, while the green man made a series of truly frightening faces, stuck out his tongue, gagged and sputtered. Was he having a heart attack? Some kind of fit?

I believe he has a frog in his throat, was Murray's diagnosis.

Sure enough, a fairly lively frog, looking none the worse for wear, popped directly out of the fellow's gaping mouth and hopped away into the woods.

"Beg pardon," the man said, completely recovered and lightly dabbing his lips with his fingers. "I didn't think it would agree with me. I said, 'I'm going to eat you.' And it said, 'Oh, no, you're not.' I don't like arguments. I'm not confrontational at all. I'm not anything."

He's very well-spoken for vegetation, observed Murray, *but he has low self-esteem. Perhaps he needs some fertilizer*.

"What do you mean, 'You're not anything'?" asked Olivier.

"I'm nothing," he said, sighing loudly and making a

sound like wind rustling leaves. He looked terribly distressed and Olivier felt he had better head him off with some encouragement before he started weeping again.

"But you're such a lovely colour, you must be something. Something very interesting, I'd say. Maybe even unique."

"A bird?"

"Well, no, obviously not a bird."

"A dog, then?" He spoke eagerly and stared at Olivier with such doggy earnestness that it was difficult to have to tell him otherwise.

He does have bark, ha, ha!

"Murray, put a cap on it, will you?"

"Don't say it. I'm not even a dog, am I? But you're someone, I can tell. You're a prince, aren't you?"

"Me? I'm just a boy."

"Not two boys? Twins, I've heard of those. You do talk to yourself and call yourself 'we.' That's putting on airs."

"Right, I should have introduced you to my friend here. His name's Murray."

Sheaffer.

"I didn't know you had a last name, Murray."

Only one of a great many things you don't know, Olivier. Murray said this in his snootiest Park Avenue script, for he had not liked being told to put a cap on it.

"I don't have a last name," moaned the green man. "Or a first name. Or a middle name, a nickname, a pet name, a given name, or even a taken name. I'm nobody, you see."

As he spoke, his voice got lower and lower until finally it sank into a damp subterranean sob.

Olivier felt very sorry for him and, while he was anxious to get on with their journey and especially anxious to find Poe, he didn't see how they could leave him in such a state.

"Your parents must have given you a name when you were born. Maybe you've simply forgotten it."

The green man gazed down at his feet for a moment and said, dismally, "I have no roots." An obvious, yet apparently cruel fact, as it provoked another great flood of tears.

Good grief, let's give him one then, before he over-waters himself. He'll rot if he keeps on like this.

"What? A name?"

Why not? Nothing easier, is there? He can have anything he likes. He can even have it in writing. How about "Jacques Plante"? Or "Johnny Bower"?

"Murray, that's brilliant."

Yes, isn't it?

"We want to give you a name," said Olivier happily, knowing it would be a wonderful gift.

The man raised his head, his cheeks all wet, and gaped at them. "A … a … name? For free?"

"Of course."

"For *keeps*?"

"As long as you want it."

"A name," he said dreamily. "My very own name. I'd *be* somebody then."

"Here." Olivier reached into his pants pocket,

intending to offer him something to dry his tears, but all he could find was the doily, which unfurled as he pulled it out. The forgotten dagger fell to the ground with a light *thump*. The sight of it had an electrifying effect on the green man. He gasped loudly, leapt to his feet and ran off into the woods, shrieking, "It wasn't me. I didn't do it! I'm no one, no one...."

Hmph. What an oddball. And I'd thought up some highly suitable names, too.

Olivier bent down to retrieve the dagger. "This terrified him," he said, studying it once more, puzzled. "He recognized it, even though I found it in the parlour."

"Herb", for example. He certainly looked like a "Herb" to me. "Herb Green". Or "Forrest", you have to admit that sounds nice. Yes, I like that.

"Look, Murray, he dropped something."

He did? Not a name, I suppose.

"It looks like some sort of toy." Olivier wrapped the dagger again and slipped it back into his pocket, then picked up the fallen object. "It's made of bone," he said, examining it more closely, "a bird's wishbone."

A former dinner companion, no doubt.

"I guess I'd better keep it for him." Olivier slid the wishbone into his pocket too. "We might run into him again up ahead. I sure would like to ask him about the dagger. I wonder what he knows that we don't?"

Not much, I'd venture.

They continued along the path, Olivier moving briskly into a generous splash of light that had brightened the forest gloom. He thought again about the game board they had discovered while searching for the hagoday. Were *they* the newest game pieces on it, being moved forward this very moment by invisible hands? What if the board was an exact model of the forest they were walking through — in the same way that the game piece he'd seen was a model for the real green man they'd just met. Given what had been depicted on the game board, where would a person named Sylvan Blink be found? Probably in the cottage located in a clearing not at all far ahead, if he remembered correctly. He supposed that's where Poe was headed as well. He picked up speed and was almost running now. Overhead, the leaves in the canopy of poplars he was passing under began *tap tapping* together in a light breeze, like small green hands applauding.

EIGHT

The nameplate that swung above the cottage door bulged with information. It read:

Dr. Sylvan Blink, B.A., M.A., Ph.D.,
Dr.Sc., M.L.S., LL.D., Dendrologist,
Speleologist, Lunarian, Superscripter,
Auteur, Gentleman, Hail Fellow Well Met,
All-Round Specialist.

"Gosh," gasped Olivier, duly impressed.

The cottage sat in a small clearing into which sunlight spilled like honey into a bowl. After spending so long in the forest, Olivier had to blink rapidly himself as he read Sylvan Blink's sign and as he took in his surroundings. Wildflowers, grasses, vines, all flourished here as profusely as the doctor's apparent abilities and accomplishments. The cottage was overgrown with Virginia creeper, buffeted on all sides by wild rose bushes, crowned with tufts of Timothy in the eaves and even trailed a smoke plant from the chimney. Apparently the cottage's clever resident laid no claim to the arts of pruning or grass cutting.

It really didn't matter to Olivier what the place looked like — he was simply glad to have found it. That path through the forest had taken many cunning twists and turns. It had split like a "Y," rounded on itself like an "O," dipped and curved like a "U." *You could almost spell yourself through it,* Murray had joked. Before his mood turned black, that is, and he began to grumble, *Some scavenger hunters — we can't even find our way.* But whether by happenstance, sharp thinking or fate, here they were standing beneath Dr. Blink's sign and drinking in a delicious hot-buttered, cinnamon-toast fragrance that was wafting through the screen door, along with a strange lilting music.

Rap on the door, lad, don't be shy. I happily conclude that we are in the presence of breakfast.

Olivier did just that, tapping smartly on the door frame, which made it rattle pleasantly. The music stopped, a chair creaked, footsteps approached. A genial face appeared on the other side of the screen, that of a puckish silver-haired boy, who looked to be about 10 years old. Olivier was a bit taken aback — this was no bearded, bespectacled, kindly old scholar.

"Excuse me," Olivier said. "We're here to see a Dr. Blink. Is he in?"

"Then you're here to see me," answered the boy. "You must be Olivier. And Murray Sheaffer," he nodded respectfully. "Do come in, I've been expecting you."

"*You're* Sylvan Blink?" Olivier didn't mean to sound quite so flummoxed, but *all those degrees*. He was just a kid!

"Most of them are honorary," Sylvan replied modestly, an amused glint in his eye for having so easily read Olivier's thoughts. He held the door open. "Please make yourselves at home. I'll brew up some fresh coffee and open a nice bottle of ink." He gestured to a comfy looking chair by the fireplace, then disappeared into the kitchen where they soon heard him rattling cups and grinding coffee beans.

"How can it be?" Olivier whispered urgently to Murray, as they settled in the chair. "How old *is* he?"

Before them, on a table busy with half-written musical scores and other papers, sat a roundish perforated instrument that looked like a cross between a flute and a potato. Presumably this is what had produced the strange music they'd heard while standing at the door. Not only could Sylvan play the thing, but he'd probably made it, too.

Possibly he is very well preserved. Murray didn't seem to be bothered by their host's extreme youth. *Look at me, well over 80 and I'm as fit and handsome as the day I was first assembled.*

"A *doctor*," persisted Olivier. "*And* he was expecting us. Pretty suspicious, I'd say." He glanced around the room, which was fairly cluttered, but tellingly so; it had the active untidiness of a person with many interests, rather than the careless messiness of a person with none. It looked familiar, too, really familiar. Shoals of books, games, fossil and insect collections, a pogo stick … wait a minute. The furniture, the carpet, the fireplace — the same! The only thing conspicuously different about it was the absence of cats … and, speaking of cats, what on earth had happened to Poe and Bliss?

"They *were* here a moment ago," said Sylvan, carrying in a large tray, heavy with clinking cutlery and china and piled high with crustless sandwiches, cinnamon buns and fancy little cakes. The sight of it made Olivier almost immediately forgive Sylvan for reading his mind — just as Sylvia seemed to do — and for being a whiz in the kitchen on top of everything else.

"Bliss arrived first," he continued, "then Poe some time after. That's how I knew you were coming."

Naturally the cats spoke to him, thought Olivier.

"I'm afraid I must have driven them away with my music. Don't worry, they won't have gone far. Have you ever played an ocarina?" He indicated the perforated potato. "I'm scoring a piece for ocarina, oud, saxophone and sistrum. Fascinating. Cream and sugar? Help yourself to the food. You must be starving. Murray, I found some vintage Quink in the cupboard, a very good year. Let me pour you some."

Too kind, Murray sighed, his words almost light enough to drift off the page.

Olivier stared intently into his cup. He didn't know about Sylvan Blink but, personally, he was too young for coffee, this coffee anyway, which was thick enough to plant a stake in. "You know," he said, raising his eyes to meet Sylvan's, "I've been in this room before. Or one almost identical to it."

Sylvan seemed genuinely surprised. "A room like *mine*?"

"Yeah. I thought you might already know about it." *Since you seem to know everything else*, he refrained from saying. "It's in Cat's Eye Corner."

"Cat's Eye Corner? You mean that old haunted house in the woods?"

"What?" Now it was Olivier's turn to be surprised. "It's not haunted. That is, I suppose it *could* be, if you believe in that sort of thing. People do live there. I do, for one, for the summer anyway."

"So she was telling the truth. For once."

"Who was?" Olivier took a good bite out of a pastry that was iced to look like a deck of cards.

"Linnet. She went in on a dare, claimed to have seen all kinds of weird things. No one believed her."

"And who is Linnet?"

"Nobody. Only a girl." Sylvan said this so dismissively that Olivier had to stifle a laugh. For the first time since their arrival, he began to relax. Despite all of Sylvan's learning, he was just a boy after all.

"What colour are her eyes?"

"Blue. Why would you want to know that?"

"Because someone with blue eyes, or one blue eye anyway, was spying on me through the keyhole of my bedroom door."

"The sneak."

"I didn't manage to catch her; she must move incredibly fast."

"Like the wind."

Sylvan's attention was diverted to the musical scores on the table, though his thoughts were obviously ranging elsewhere, as were Olivier's. This Linnet person didn't sound like "just a girl" to him. For one thing, she'd have to be braver than most to go into what was considered a haunted house. He yawned hugely, suddenly remembering that he hadn't slept at all the previous night. His eyelids felt as if they had sinkers attached to them. He stared at his cup, still full of that vile black coffee, wondering if he should hazard a sip, then reached for the sugar bowl and popped a handful of sugar cubes into his mouth instead.

Murray, meanwhile, had rolled himself halfway across the table. He had that agitated "look" that meant he was itching to express an opinion. Olivier picked him up, but before he could transfer him to the notebook Murray began to scrawl something on the sheet music. Olivier wondered if this wasn't a bit rude of him, but then saw that he was writing musical notes and not the stiff little characters you usually see, either. These notes had a certain off-duty quality to them and were balancing and swinging on the musical staff like a bunch of partying acrobats.

"That's great," exclaimed Sylvan. "He's composing something. Can you read music, Olivier?"

"Some. I took piano lessons for a while. These notes do look sort of familiar."

"Yes, and look, he's adding some lyrics. Oh, I believe he's singing."

Gonna sit right down and write myself a lettterrrrr.

"Um, I wonder what's gotten into him?"

"Dear me. Too much Quink and on an empty barrel, too. He's positively inked."

The boys looked at one another and started to laugh. *Har, har*, chimed in Murray, and that made them laugh even more.

Unfortunately, their fun was short-lived. A hard object hit the front window of the cottage with a loud *thump* and enough force to make a tentacled crack in the glass.

"What was that?" Sylvan leapt out of his chair.

"Sounded like a bird hitting the window." Olivier, too, jumped to his feet, but not before scooping Murray up and placing him back in his shirtfront pocket. He didn't want to leave him alone in his present state. What if he were to roll off the table and hurt himself?

Once outside, they searched the area directly below the window and found, not the poor stunned bird that Olivier expected to see, but a crunched wad of paper, about the size of a small child's fist, clumsily taped together and weighted with something heavy. When Sylvan tore off the tape and unwrapped it, they saw that it was a large marble made of clear glass, with a swirl of deep red in its centre — a tiny floating scarf of scarlet.

"What a beauty," gasped Sylvan, staring at it with fascination as he handed the paper wrapper to Olivier.

It was a message of some sort. *This*, and not the marble, was the significant thing here. Olivier read it, realizing quickly that it was the kind of message that struck horror into the hearts of parents — the spelling was atrocious. (His spelling, of course, was always impekable ... impecabel ... or, put more simply, perfect.)

restorr Dirk
if knot
kats wil dye
And i meen it!
yors trewly
Sputum

CAPTAN UF SO-SO GANG

"I can't believe it. This is incredible," said Sylvan.

"Who is this guy? He can't be serious?"

"Serious? Do you know how long I've been searching for one of these?" Sylvan held the marble up to the light to admire it more fully. "Amazing," he said.

"Sylvan, *forget* the marble." Olivier rattled the paper under his nose. "This is about Bliss and Poe! They've been catnapped or something. Here, read it."

"*Tsk, tsk,*" Sylvan murmured as he read it. "Bogus spelling." He then handed it back to Olivier, saying, "I wouldn't worry about it."

"What!"

"Bliss and Poe are far smarter than anyone in the So-So Gang, especially Sputum. He's all splutter and no action. I expect the cats are teasing them, pretending to go along with their foolish plan."

"Who is this Dirk mentioned in the note? A friend of yours?"

"You've heard of Excalibur, haven't you?"

"Sure, that's the name of King Arthur's sword."

"And Sting?"

"Bilbo Baggins' dagger. Are you telling me that Dirk is a ... weapon?"

"That's right. Dirk is a dirk. Dirk Smith, if you want its full name. It's a dagger, quite deadly. It's gone missing, you see, which has caused a lot of trouble. The So-So Gang have practically declared war on Linnet, who they assume has it, and she suspects Mr. Mirific, with good cause I might add. He's always cooking something up. Now I suppose they think *I* have it. What a bother."

"You don't."

"I know."

"*I* do."

"You *do*?"

But before Olivier could triumphantly produce the dagger, or dirk, he heard a *zinging* sound high in the air ... and then he hit the ground, knocked flat on his back. He had been felled by an arrow, a slight pencil-size one, but lethal nonetheless. It hit him in the chest, perilously close to his heart, and he appeared to be seriously wounded — blood was flowing freely.

Horrified, Sylvan swiftly bent to staunch the flow. But it wasn't blood that was staining his fingers — it was ink — ink of a deep and mortal red.

Murray, silenced in Olivier's shirtfront pocket, had taken the blow.

NINE

Once again Olivier found himself wandering in the
great Drak Woulds, only this time he was alone.
How he missed seeing his dear friend's voice.
He knew that he would gladly withstand any amount
of nattering, if only Murray were with him. Olivier had
gotten so used to their notebook chitchat that now
his writing hand felt empty and useless, haunted by
Murray's absence.

By mid-afternoon, when the cats still hadn't
returned and Sylvan admitted that he too was getting
worried, Olivier decided that he couldn't wait any
longer — he had to find this so-called So-So Gang and
hand Dirk over. He didn't *want* to, never before having
had in his possession anything quite so fascinating, but
it wasn't worth the risk.

He had hated leaving Murray behind, but his pen

pal was in no shape to travel. In fact, his shape had taken quite a beating. Sylvan had tended Murray's wounded frame, but not his spirits. He still lay inert, cold as any inanimate object. Sylvan assured Olivier that he would come around — it was simply a matter of time. Secretly they both prayed that this would be so.

"If you decide to go," Sylvan had said earlier, "I promise to stay by Murray's side and keep constant watch over him. But *do* be careful," he warned. "I wouldn't have thought the So-Sos capable — nothing like that has ever happened here before. You could be walking straight into a trap."

Olivier had felt trapped anyway, pacing back and forth, so he finally asked Sylvan to draw him a map showing the way to the So-So Gang's headquarters. ("Hindquarters is more like it," said Sylvan.) He could easily get there and back before nightfall — if all went smoothly. Sylvan also gave him the marble.

"No, you keep it," Olivier had insisted. "I know you want it and I have loads at home, really."

"I have a feeling it was meant for you. Sputum wouldn't have the foggiest, but I think he sent you something you'll need."

Olivier took the marble and, holding it briefly up to the light, noticed that there was something unusual about it, though he couldn't quite say what.

"Thanks," he said, fishing in his pocket to draw out the three marbles he had brought with him. He gave these to Sylvan. "Not much of a trade, I'm afraid."

"They're great. I wonder what they do."

"Do?"

"Never mind, you'd better get going. You don't want to get caught in the forest at night."

Olivier set out and was soon deep in the woods, passing by trees that were as familiar to him as his own name — spruce, tamarack, birch. The late-afternoon sun burnished their rustling leaves and dappled the path before him with shifting patterns of light. He found it hard to believe that he wasn't simply walking along some wooded trail near home, keeping his eye peeled for chipmunks, snakes and, if lucky, a salamander. But he'd better believe it, because in a place like this you might encounter anything.

He also thought these So Sos sounded a bit lame. Still, he was feeling nervous about confronting them, a whole gang, after all. He resolved to keep his wits about him, no matter what.

As he progressed farther into the forest, the leafy canopy overhead wove itself together more tightly, soon entirely obscuring the patches of blue sky above. Before long he came to a place where the path forked, splitting in two different directions. When he got out the map to see which path he should follow, a sudden puff of wind shushed in his ear, lifted a strand of his hair and plucked the paper clean out of his hands. He watched, astounded, as it swirled away from him, borne by this sudden breeze into the depths of the forest. What was he supposed to do now? Get lost? Which is precisely what he did.

After losing the map Olivier stepped up his pace, knowing that his chances of finding his way without it would soon die with the light. He considered returning to Sylvan's cottage, but decided instead to press on. Then the path he was on abruptly ended. He had taken a wrong turn somewhere, so doubled back. Chancing a shortcut through the underbrush, his foot caught an exposed root and he fell, scraping his elbow, raking his face with a sharp branch and frightening a nesting grouse that shot up with a screeching flurry of feathers. When he found what he thought was the main path again, it didn't look at all familiar and he had no idea which way to go.

Night fell like a guillotine, relentless and swift. With it went, if not his head, then certainly his reason. He blamed himself for losing the map, for deserting Murray and for failing the cats. Not only that — it was lonely and scary in the woods and he was hungry and sore and tired.

As he was hanging his head so low, Olivier couldn't help but notice that his pocket had begun to glow with a small light. The light was blinking off and on, which made him think that a firefly must have crawled inside, lost, like himself. He slid his hand into his pocket, carefully reaching toward it. What he drew out was not a firefly, but the cat's-eye. Holding it up between his two fingers, it shot piercing beams this way and that, probing the dark with a "seeing" kind of light. Almost immediately it settled its light beam on a clump of bushes several paces behind him. Olivier stepped over to them and swept back a spray of branches with his free hand. The bushes concealed another path, an offshoot of the main one he now remembered from the map. Eliot had told him that the cat's-eye might come in handy, but this was amazing. It was actually giving him directions as well as lighting the way, guiding him like a visual compass or a seeing-eye dog minus the dog.

Blessed now with the gem's night vision — a portable third eye — Olivier moved quickly along a network of forest trails. He couldn't guess how the luminous stone worked, but it knew where he wanted to go. He felt hopeful again, his confidence restored, except for a persistent and nagging feeling that he was being followed. Several times the cat's-eye sent its thin laser beam of light flying off the path to search among the undergrowth, as if it too were trying to catch sight of a dark prowling presence. Once, on a branch directly above him, he could have sworn that he saw a quick flash of eyes and heard the branch itself groan, as if a menacing weight had suddenly lifted.

If he were being shadowed, Olivier didn't have much time to worry about it. He could hear the low din of voices ahead and see the glow of a campfire. The voices were chanting something, a poem by the sounds of it, although he couldn't make out the words. With the cat's-eye sharply focused, he crept closer, stepping off the path and circling around, until he was in a good position to view the proceedings. A group of children were marching around a sputtering campfire — he couldn't see what

they were burning, but it didn't look like logs — and
half-heartedly intoning:

We're sorta horrible and kinda cruel,
not bad looking, not everybody's fool.
We're a little of this and a little of that,
we got no opinions, we got no hats.
We're iffy and shifty and not very nifty.
We like our grub half-baked.
Our lives are bland, our laughter's canned,
got no appetites to slake.
Mediocrity's our philosophy.
Tedium's our medium.
We're the So-So Gang, if you wanna know,
middle of the road, the only way to go.

Losers, thought Olivier. Under normal circumstances,
he'd feel sorry for these kids, the kind to be overlooked at
school, last to be chosen, considered a joke, if considered
at all. But these were not normal circumstances. Forget
the nerdy haircuts, the droning nasal voices, they had
clearly been tormenting the cats and not only with bad
poetry. There they were — Poe and Bliss — tied to a tree
trunk with thickly, if clumsily, knotted rope and looking
very odd, very *pink* to be exact. Their fur was bristled
and stiff and ... *pink*. Olivier had to fight the urge to step
out of his hiding place and tell the gang off, but he knew
it would be wiser to wait.

After finishing their lacklustre ritual, the gang seated
themselves in a circle around the fire. Olivier half-
expected them to start singing goofy camp songs. One

of the group, a tall gangly kid, had remained standing and he now stuck out his hand, held it flat and rocked it slightly back and forth in what you might call a So-So signal or salute. The others seated around the fire responded likewise.

"So," the one standing said, "such is the insalubrious situation."

Olivier knew that the speaker had to be Sputum for the obvious reason that when he spoke, flecks of spittle flew out of his mouth. He was dressed in a long blue frock coat, red breeches and droopy buskins. He was also wearing a curly, blond wig that sat slightly askew on his head.

"As youse can see, we has dyed the prisoners." He made an exaggerated and wooden gesture in the general direction of the cats.

"Oh, no," Olivier groaned softly to himself, recalling the words of the ransom note, "Kats wil dye."

"Have," corrected a girl, who must have been sitting a bit too close to Sputum, for as she spoke she removed her glasses and wiped them. "We *have* dyed the prisoners."

"Wen," Sputum answered sternly, or tried to, "these is the new rules, see. I mean, you know that. So stop being, uh, so … obstreperous."

Wen ducked the spray that issued from this reprimand while grumbling, "You don't even know what the word means, you big drip."

Sputum continued (and everyone shifted back out of range), "It's blinkingly, blisteringly, boilingly…

blatant, yeah, that something more is gotta be done."

"Pull their whiskers," ventured a So-So.

"Yank their tails," suggested another.

"Nah, chuck 'em in the fire."

"That's it. Roast 'em. Fry 'em."

Olivier might have been more alarmed at this nasty turn of events if the So-Sos had spoken with any real conviction, but they didn't sound overly eager to do any of these things.

"HE would like that, yes-s-s-s-s-s-s!" The fire hissed and spit along with Sputum, like a backup chorus.

"If we did it, would HE give us our glasses back?" asked a pale and very timid-looking boy.

"Craven, listen up, we don't need 'em any more, *eh*? Glasses is for goofballs and weaklings and weaselly *readers*." Here Sputum glared at Wen, who glared right back, *her* glasses glinting in the firelight.

That's it, thought Olivier. Why didn't I guess? They're all short-sighted. He had noticed them squinting and screwing up their eyes, but assumed the smoke from the fire was getting to them. It was going to be a snap to rescue the cats. He would sneak behind the gang and use Dirk to cut through the ropes. No point handing the dagger over if he didn't have to, especially to this crew. They might hurt themselves.

It was an excellent plan, simple and straightforward, and it might even have worked if someone hadn't beaten him to it. This someone, quick and agile as a monkey, leapt down out of the trees, untied the ropes with uncanny speed, scooped the cats into a sack, then climbed back up and was off again, disappearing into the treetops before anyone could say, "Stop her!"

Sputum *was* trying to say it, but he was so befuddled and tongue-tied that, honestly, for once he couldn't spit it out. And Olivier couldn't say it, because *he* was jumped from behind and a huge asphyxiating hand clamped over his mouth. The next thing he knew, he was being lifted up, up into the trees, struggling and kicking, as much against sleep as against his captor, for suddenly he felt waves of warm dreamy darkness washing over him. Below, the circle of So-Sos sat blinking and straining to see what was going on, wondering if something out of the ordinary had happened and if, as usual, they had missed it.

TEN

Disconnected words were bobbing like corks in Olivier's head. He felt a breeze playing about his face, actually *playing*, for it eddied on his brow, slid down his nose and used his chin as a diving board to leap lightly onto his chest. The boat was rocking gently, creaking.... He opened his eyes cautiously, experimentally, and immediately the teasing wind dropped, as though caught in the act. He *was* on a boat. He was stretched out on a bunk bed, top level, in a boat's cabin. The cabin was small and snug, fitted with plenty of brass, as well as a couple of barrels, a sea chest and what looked like a stack of charts in one corner.

Why was the porthole a deep green with leaves pressing against it? And that scratching noise? It was the same sound he'd heard in his bedroom at Cat's Eye Corner — the sound of branches brushing and scraping against the window. He reached down to check his pockets. Empty! He sat up quickly, too quickly, because he thumped his head on a low beam and sank back down with a groan.

"Sit still," a voice ordered.

Olivier propped himself up on an elbow to see who was speaking. It was that girl who had practically flown down out of the trees to capture the cats. She was seated on a bench in the ship's galley, carving a stick of wood with a penknife. She had dark wind-tangled hair and a scowling expression that made her look quarrelsome. Or so Olivier thought, not being much in the mood for good first impressions.

"What have you done with the cats?" he demanded. "And the things that were in my pocket?"

She set down her whittling and stared at him for a long moment. Her eyes were blue, light and sharp. One of those eyes, he knew for sure, had observed him before.

"You mean this?" She flicked open her palm to reveal the cat's-eye. "This ... sunstone?"

"What?"

She gave him a sly, satisfied look. "You didn't know did you, that 'cat's-eyes' are also called 'sunstones'?"

"You're right, I didn't." Obviously, she had done a lot of spying (more than he'd done) and knew all about the scavenger hunt. "I'll tell you what I *do* know. I'm taking my stuff and leaving. And I can see why Sylvan doesn't like you, too." So saying, Olivier leapt off the bunk. But before his feet could even touch the ground, a sudden swirling wind caught him in mid-air, tumbled him once, twice, then dumped him on the floor with a *thud*.

"My gosh, what happened? *What* was that?" One look at her laughing face told him. "*You*? But *how*?"

"Easy," she said, snapping her fingers. He felt himself being lifted into the air as if by invisible hands. He was gently shaken, like a wrinkled shirt, then set on his feet.

"Whoa! If you're a magician, you're an awfully good one." He couldn't spot any concealed trickery in the cabin, air-blowing vents in the floor, that sort of thing.

"I'm not a magician," she said. "I'm only a *girl*, remember, and Sylvan doesn't like me because I can do some things he can't."

"Sorry." He'd struck a nerve. "You know, you did mess up my plans to rescue the cats. You've been snooping around, too, and spying."

"And I stole your map when you were in the woods. And, before that, I shot you."

"*You* shot me?" Of course, it was an *arrow* she had been carving with her penknife, he should have realized that.

"Yes."

"But you could have killed me!"

"*Could* have, if I'd wanted to. I knew the arrow would deflect off that pen in your pocket, the same one you're always scribbling with. You a reporter or something?"

"*That* was Murray." Talk about striking a nerve — he was furious.

"Murray?"

"My friend. I can't believe you'd do that to him."

"Your friend? How ... weird."

"Wait a minute, you live in a boat in the trees (he'd peeked out of the nearest porthole and confirmed that this was certainly true), you've got some sort of strange powers, you hurt people *and* pens, for fun, and you call what *I* do weird?"

"It *was* fun," she said matter-of-factly. "I loved the look on Sylvan's face when I flattened you. I didn't know about your friend, though, honest. Is he all right?"

"I don't know." She seemed sincere. "I hope so."

"I was only trying to help."

"Help? I don't see how."

"By proving to you that you'll never find the things on your scavenger hunt list without me. You don't even recognize them when you do find them. Like this one." She made that flicking motion with her hand again and into it, out of nowhere, dropped the bone object that Olivier had found after the green man had run off into the woods. "I used to have one of these when I was little. It's a skipjack."

"Come on, I know what a skipjack is. A fish, or a kind of beetle."

"Yeah, but it's a kind of sailboat too, as well as a foolish person (not unlike Sputum), and it's a toy made out of a bird's wishbone — *this* toy right here."

"I suppose you're going to tell me that the marble

Sylvan gave me is on the list as well? Though called something else, naturally."

"Naturally." And just as naturally — or was it supernaturally — she raised a finger and the marble appeared, rolling out from under a bench, across the floor and into her open hand.

"How do you *do* that?" Olivier marvelled.

"Oh, it's just the wind," she said. "Air currents, you know. My family have always worked with wind — navigators, flutists, kite makers. But look, this is far more interesting." She held the marble up to the light, as Sylvan had done. "See the red swirling around inside? It's moving."

Olivier stepped closer. "Are you doing that?"

"Not me. These are rare. I wonder where those useless So-Sos got it?"

They both stared at the marble, fascinated, watching the streak of red within the clear glass shifting into different patterns, drifting, circulating like … like what?

"Blood," exclaimed Olivier. "It's a blood."

"Right."

"I have a marble at home like this one, except the inside doesn't move. It's called a 'ketchup.'"

"Funny name."

"Speaking of which," he said, "isn't your name 'Sparrow' or 'Oriole' or something?"

She laughed aloud at this, which sent a bolt of air skimming past his ears. "It's Linnet," she said.

"OK, Linnet," he replied, "where are the cats and when am I going to see them?"

"As soon as I can see Dirk Smith. It was a good idea to hide it, by the way."

"I didn't. You mean it wasn't in my pocket with the other stuff? It was wrapped in a doily."

"This thing?" Linnet reached into her own pocket and pulled out the doily. When she held it up and let it drop, it floated slowly down on a cushion of air, then rearranged itself quite nicely, doily-wise, on the galley table.

"Yes, that's it. But where's the dagger? I can't have lost it. I know I still had it when I reached the So-Sos' camp because I felt it in my pocket when I put the cat's-eye, I mean sunstone, back."

Linnet thought for a moment, then let out a big sigh, which caused a wind chime suspended from the ceiling to tinkle softly. "I knew it," she said, sounding disappointed. "I shouldn't have trusted him."

"Who?"

"My apprentice. Ex-apprentice, I guess. He's the one who knocked you out with that herbal soporific and carried you up here." She then added, "He's a woodwose."

"A woodwose," Olivier repeated.

"We think that's what he is. That's what the Two Holies say, anyway."

"The *who*?"

"Look, I'll fill you in later, but right now we've got to try and stop him. Grab your treasures; they won't be safe here. You're not the only scavenger in these woods, you know. We'll take the high way."

He stuffed the sunstone, skipjack, blood *and* doily back into his pocket. (And where, pray tell, were his string ball and package of gum?) He followed Linnet out onto the deck, then watched as she stepped nimbly from the bow of the boat onto a nearby branch and from that onto another and another. Ah, *that* high way. She moved swiftly and surefooted along a network of branches — a pathway through the trees. Olivier didn't hesitate for a second, but followed right after. Good thing he was a practised tree climber. Good thing he wasn't afraid of heights (well, not very). Good thing he didn't look down.

ELEVEN

S ome of the branches were trunk-thick and stable, easy enough to negotiate, while other, thinner ones wobbled dangerously as he inched along them. It made him feel like a high-wire performer in a circus — with no safety net below, either. He was careful to avoid any cracked or dead branches, recalling a tree-climbing cousin of his who hadn't been so alert and ended up with a broken leg. The real problem was keeping pace with Linnet. She must have travelled this way hundreds of times and seemed to fly along, with the wind gambolling like a puppy at her heels.

A couple of times Olivier had to wedge his foot into the fork of a tree in order to climb to a higher branch and once his shoe got stuck and came right off. "Darn!" he said, practically hanging upside down to retrieve it. If Linnet got too far ahead, he would lose sight of her.

She was really going slower than usual to keep an eye on him, but didn't make a big production of it.

"Where are we going?" he managed to shout when she was within earshot.

"You'll see."

He knew he must be in the thick of it now, which is exactly what he wanted, but he couldn't help think that adventures might benefit from a recess. Times like this, with deer flies dive-bombing and muscles aching and hands slick with sweat and throat parched and stomach grumbling ... a guy could use a time out. As he climbed and stretched and strained, ever mindful of keeping his balance, Olivier thought of his cozy room at home and his nice warm bed. He pictured himself snuggled comfortably in it, his tape player on one side, his *Tintin* collection on the other, while clattering sounds drifted up from downstairs as his parents fixed dinner. He wondered if they knew he was missing from Cat's Eye Corner and if Gramps was worried. (He suspected that Sylvia wouldn't be.) Maybe this was going to be one of those adventures in which no time actually passes in the "real" world and the hero arrives back expecting everyone to be worried sick and it turns out no one has even noticed that he was gone.

When he spotted Linnet resting up ahead, leaning against the broad trunk of an old oak, Olivier guessed that they must have finally come to the end of their treetop journey. It was an exciting route, but he'd be happy to get his feet on solid ground again. Moving closer, he saw that a huge space yawned between the branch she was standing on and his own.

"It's all right," she said, aware of his hesitation. "You can do it."

"Are you kidding? I can't jump that far."

"Sure you can."

"Easy for you to say. Why don't I climb down, walk over, then climb up the tree you're in?"

"You can't. There's a ravine below overgrown with Devil's Walking Stick. You'd get shredded."

"Guess I'll have to turn back, then."

"Hey, you're supposed to be the hero here, aren't you?"

"Yeah, but I'm a sensible hero. Okay, okay, here goes. I hope you're prepared to pick up the pieces."

Olivier studied the branch, then concentrated on the spot where he had to land. He might be able to make it, just. Nervously, he slipped his hands into his pockets and absentmindedly drew out the skipjack. Without waiting another second, he jumped. He flew through the air, legs pedalling madly and landed right *smack* beside Linnet.

"You did it!" She grabbed his shoulders to steady him.

"You helped me, didn't you?" he panted.

"I might have, if you'd needed it."

He turned the skipjack over in his hand, appraising the bone toy. *Nah*, he said to himself and pocketed it once again.

They continued on through the trees for a short while, then made a rapid descent down a red maple and jumped to the ground. They had arrived at a river. Linnet began walking up and down the riverbank, kicking at the weeds and muttering to herself.

Olivier picked up a stone and threw it into the water. The river, flowing lazily along, accepted the stone with the merest *plink*. He began searching around for another nice flat one, good for skipping, when, strangely, the first stone he'd thrown landed right back at his feet. *Plunk*. Olivier looked up in surprise. Linnet was still fully absorbed in her own search; clearly, she hadn't thrown anything. Olivier scanned the far bank, then the river itself. No one. He moved closer and tried to peer down into the water's depths, but all he saw was his own reflection, shimmering on the surface, smiling and waving at him. *What!* He craned his neck, widened his eyes — surely he was seeing things — but his reflection continued to float before him and was moving its lips as if speaking. Then, with a silent laugh, it shrugged its shoulders and vanished, rippling outward as a reflection does when a stone lands in the centre of it.

"Linnet!" he shouted.

"Olivier!" she shouted back.

"What?" they both said, as if speaking in echoes.

"Here," she said, "in this muddy patch — footprints — big ones and cat tracks, too. So he did come this way, just as I thought. Hey, what's wrong with you?"

He was about to blurt out what he'd seen when she glanced toward the river and said, "Oh hi, Fathom," casually greeting a boy who had popped his head out of the water. He squirted a high arching stream of water through his pursed lips, fountain-style. "I hope you haven't been playing tricks on my friend," she added.

Fathom laughed, a merry lilting sound like a spring chuckling over rocks, and swam toward them. When he clambered onto the bank, Olivier saw that he was dressed in a kind of wet suit, but one of a finer, less rubbery material, with skin-tight leggings and a vest that had the exact colouring and markings of a leopard frog. His skin was the white of a frog's throat, his hair and lashes were the glossy golden shade of a frog's eyelids and he had webs between his fingers and toes. He *was* a boy, but a curiously amphibious one.

Linnet quickly introduced them, then got down to business. "Fathom, we have to find the woodwose. He was here, wasn't he? Did you see him?"

"Sure, he was here. He dumped a couple of cats out of a sack into the river. They didn't like it, I can tell you that," he said, delighted. "They howled and yowled, then swam straight over to the other bank and ran off through the woods. Then the woodwose started to howl and yowl and tear leaves out of his hair. I don't think he expected them to swim."

"Trying to clean them up, I guess. The So-So Gang were holding them ransom, to get Dirk Smith from Olivier, but because they're so, so, you know, stupid, they thought 'dye' was the same as 'die' and anyway what matters is that the woodwose has Dirk."

"Tadpoles!" he said, which was Fathom's version of "Yikes!"

"Do you think he'll hand Dirk over to HIM?"

"He'd be too scared, wouldn't he?"

"I don't know. Which way did he go from here?"

Fathom pointed upriver to a densely overgrown stretch of the bank. "He probably didn't want to come back to you empty-handed is all. I bet he's hiding somewhere."

"Yeah, but that's the right direction if he was heading to HIS place. HE's got to be behind this somehow."

Olivier was trying his best to follow this conversation, but who was HE, the guy who always got the capitals? He bent down to pick up the stone again, the one he'd thrown into the river, and began tossing it from hand to hand, half-listening to the others, but mostly thinking about Poe and Bliss. He was relieved to know that they had escaped unharmed and hoped they weren't lost. A picture of the cats slowly appeared in his head, as clear and detailed as a photograph, showing them curled up together, tucked as snug as yin and yang. They were fast asleep in a bed of grass and wildflowers, a tossed salad of chewed catnip leaves strewn around them. This image was suddenly replaced by another, of the green man. He was on the run, desperately pawing through a thicket of bracken, an eager and pitiful expression on his face. Olivier gripped the stone hard and said, "HE promised him a name."

"*Yes*, that's it." Linnet stared at Olivier, surprised. "In exchange for Dirk, Mr. Mirific must have promised the woodwose something he wants more than anything — a name. How did *you* know?"

"I didn't. I don't. *This* does, somehow." He opened his hand and showed them the stone.

"Brain coral!" Linnet exclaimed. "You found it! That's terrific. You're getting better at this game."

Fathom grinned at him and winked, so what could Olivier do but nod and say, "Absolutely!"

TWELVE

"You should try some, Olivier." Linnet was bending down over the riverbank scooping water into her cupped palm.

"Is it safe?"

"More than that, it's delicious. And filling, like a seven-course meal."

Olivier didn't see how water could taste like anything but water or fill anybody up. Making a ladle out of his hand, he dipped it into the river. He took a wary, miserly sip, rolled the water around in his mouth as if he were a wine taster and concluded, "Chicken soup." He stared at the clear drips still clinging to his fingers, then reached down again for another, less cautious, sampling. "Poached salmon," he said, "new potatoes and baby carrots smothered in parsley butter, Portuguese bread, a salad, Brie, plums," and several satisfying handfuls later, "chocolate cake." A toothpick conveniently floated by and he snatched it up before falling back on the riverbank, replete.

"How come your rivers are like restaurants?" he asked, trying to pick the water out of his teeth, assuredly a tricky *and* a trickly business.

"That sounds like a riddle," said Linnet. "They're not usually, you know. Ma Flood must have cooked up a feast when Fathom told her we were waiting around up here. She's a great hostess. Sometimes she turns the river into ginger ale and throws a big party. You should see the fish jump then."

Ma Flood was Fathom's mother, as Olivier had discovered when they were making plans to check out Mr. Mirific's place. The idea was to rescue Dirk and the woodwose, if they were there, and to generally try to find out what was going on. Once they had decided that travelling by river would provide the quickest route, Fathom volunteered a raft for the trip, a derelict but serviceable one he'd found caught in the reeds that very morning. The only snag in this plan was that the river was flowing the wrong way.

"I'll talk to Ma," Fathom said. "Maybe she'll switch it for us. I'm sure she wouldn't mind, for a little while anyway." With that, he jackknifed into the water, cutting its surface without even a ripple, before swimming into its depths.

"He *lives* down there?" Olivier asked, trying hard to imagine such a thing. "His mother, too?"

"His whole family," Linnet said. "They're waterworkers.

Caretakers, I guess you'd call them. They keep the river in order and flowing along as it should."

"You mean they're like nixies, or naiads?"

She gave him a skeptical look. "These are real people."

"Not in *my* world. There's no such thing as water-workers. Or windworkers, for that matter."

"But this *is* your world, a corner of it. Anyway, may I see that piece of brain coral you found?"

"Sure." Olivier fished it out of his pocket and hand-ed it to her.

She examined it briefly, then squeezed it tight in her fist, at the same time squeezing her eyes shut. "*Hmph.*" She re-opened eyes and fist. "Nothing. I thought I'd see how Fathom was making out, but I guess it doesn't work for me." She handed it back to Olivier. "You try."

He enfolded the brain coral in his hand and immediately pictured Fathom seated on a couch of woven reeds in a room that looked very much like an ordinary living room, except for the school of fish swimming through it.

"He's sewing," said Olivier in surprise. He was, too. With a fishbone needle and a fibrous thread he was stitching a wavering green beard of moss onto a rock, with difficulty. "He should use a coral stitch," observed Olivier. "Do you think he's forgotten about us?"

"He wouldn't do that," said Linnet. "Ma Flood probably nabbed him for shirking his chores. Let's give him five more minutes."

"Enough time for an experiment?"

"What kind of experiment?"

"I want to see if I can jump across the river."

"What?" Linnet laughed. "Are you crazy? It must be 20 feet across."

"I think I can do it."

"Yeah? You barely made it from one tree branch to another as I recall."

"You really didn't help me earlier, right?"

"Right."

"Okay, so what's the worst thing that can happen if I don't make it?"

"You *can* swim, can't you?"

"Definitely ... sort of ... dog paddle."

Linnet gazed at him, then at the river. "The current can be pretty strong." She shook her head and muttered under her breath, "Heroes."

"Well, here goes," Olivier said, as jauntily as he could manage. He walked back a distance from the riverbank so as to have a good running start. Then, while revving his engines and pawing the ground with his feet, he exchanged the brain coral for the skipjack. Holding it aloft, he tore off at a great clip, reached the edge of the bank and — flew. At least that's how it looked to Linnet.

"Amazing!" she shouted to Olivier, who was now standing on the other side of the river, smiling in amazement himself.

"Guess I've got this one figured out," he said, waving the skipjack like a magic wand. "Watch." Again, he ran and jumped and...

up,

up,

up,   he climbed, sailing over the river, then

down

down

down,

to the other side.

Linnet ran up and clapped him heartily on the back, which was followed by a bracing gust of wind that tousled his hair into wavy peaks. "How did you know?" she asked.

"It was a hunch. Each of the scavenger hunt objects must have some particular power."

"Yes," said Linnet, more to herself than Olivier. "I wonder...."

"What the blood does. No idea."

"Courage? It might make you really brave."

"I don't need help in *that* department," said Olivier, somewhat crisply.

"Ha! I suppose we'll find out. Say, there's Fathom. He's got the raft."

"All aboard," Fathom called, head appearing above the water behind a raft as he guided it toward the bank.

Olivier eyed the creaky vessel dubiously and for the second time that day he asked, "Is it safe?"

"No," said Fathom amiably. "What's the point of that? Anyway, it's all we've got. We'd better hurry because Ma's not going to keep the river switched for long."

"Hop on," said Linnet, doing so herself. "This

shouldn't bother someone as brave as you are," she teased.

"Darn right," he said and jumped on. The raft dipped and bobbed crazily, sucking at the river and splashing water onto their feet.

"Hey," she laughed, "watch it!"

When they were ready, Fathom ferried them out to mid-river and let go, swimming alongside. Then he said, loudly, "Zeke!"

A shimmering blue form zipped past Fathom's nose, doubled back for a closer look, zoomed off again, circled around his head a couple of times and finally settled on a slick strand of his coppery hair.

"A *dragonfly*."

"Yeah, Zeke," said Fathom.

"Great." Olivier had seen plenty of dragonflies in his day — darners, hawkers, skimmers — but had never actually *met* one before. He considered them to be the stars of the insect world (they *were* flashy dressers). As the raft travelled upriver, skimming along like a leaf on a stream, Zeke entertained everybody with his aerial antics, playing tag with Fathom and, most helpfully, blazing a trail through clouds of mosquitoes.

The river slowed occasionally for them to take in points of interest — a painted turtle meditating on a log, a beaver family building a lodge. Olivier reasoned that if Ma Flood was controlling the river, she probably wanted to make the trip educational, although he couldn't help but feel a bit like a tourist.

In any event, it wasn't long before they arrived at

their destination and Fathom guided the raft into a clump of reeds.

"It's not far from here," Linnet explained. "If we sneak up on Mirific, maybe we can get some idea of what he's up to. I think you should stay with the raft, Fathom. You know what happens when you're away from the water too long."

"Aw, Linnet, I'll be okay. Besides," he said, leaping onto the bank with a neat froggy hop, "you might need my help." He swept his arm in a wide arc and a curtain of water appeared in midair, tumbling down, with silver sprats leaping out of it, and into the river. Then he was off and running, like a stream flashing through the tall grass. Zeke was next, shooting over the waving fronds like a dart.

"Quick," said Linnet and they took off after them. "But remember, Olivier," she warned, her words snapping like a banner in the wind, "be on your guard."

THIRTEEN

Thirteen, eh? Unlucky as walking under ladders, spilling salt or crossing the paths of black cats (except for one). Not that Olivier was thinking about any of this as he brushed cobwebs out of his face, a great many of which were draped and swagged over the trees, and dodged numerous spiders and bats, which he took to be real until he smacked into one. Then he saw that they were only silly plastic toys. The path he and the others were following was an obstacle course — they ran up and down ramps, zigzagged around rock piles and even jumped through hoops like trained dogs.

Eventually they arrived at a large fence painted to look like a piano keyboard. "Wow," Olivier whispered to Linnet as he peeked through a crack between the A and B notes. "It's a circus!" Like Linnet's boathouse, it was situated in the trees, but was composed of a series of pavilions with spiral domes, turrets, wildly coloured awnings, mirror windows, murals, flags, balloons, clocks, an airplane elevator device and a slick, red tongue-shaped slide that sloped to the ground from the laughing mouth of an enormous clown's face. A sign studded with flashing lights read: **WELCOME TO HODGE-PODGE LODGE, THE CONGLOMERATION CORPORATION**.

That's friendly enough, Olivier reasoned.

Another oddity then presented itself. A small man appeared at the top of the slide, shot down the length of the clown's tongue and bounced off the tip, landing several feet ahead on a lavishly decorated platform. He had a whacking great smile on his face and in his hand a megaphone, through which he immediately began to bawl, "I'm in short form at present, but I'm in **EXCELLENT** form, **SUPERLATIVE**, ha ha, present **PERFECT!**"

Huh, thought Olivier, he's full of himself.

And he was that, full to the brim — so much so, he looked as if he might burst. He had round eyes and a bulbous nose, souffléd orange hair that rose off his head like a bale of cotton candy and a tiny fedora perched on top. He wore a suit so white it hurt Olivier's eyes and its buttons strained to contain him, just as his skin seemed strained, as if he were just *too much*, even for himself. On his feet he wore snakeskin cowboy boots with clickers on the heels that made a fair amount of racket as he strode about on the platform, *clickety-click, clickety-click,* at the same time patting his own back with his free hand and periodically shouting through the megaphone, "**BRILLIANT! STUPENDOUS! AMAZING!**" When he wasn't busy congratulating himself, he was firing candy into his mouth — jelly beans, toffee, jujubes — his pockets bulged with a steady supply. He ate these greedily, except for the black licorice-flavoured candies, which he spat out, screwing up his face as he did so.

"I don't like those either," Olivier said, a bit too loudly.

"Shhhhh," warned Linnet and whether she meant to or not, her "shhhhh" once uttered became a *shush* of wind that slipped over the fence, circled around the little man, picked up his fedora and deposited it on the head of a nearby ceramic gnome.

At this he roared, "Am I to be honoured by a visit?! Oh yes, I know you're out there, kiddies. Can't slip one by **HIS OMNISCIENCE**, you know, the **GREAT MR. MIRIFIC!!**"

Mr. Insufferable was more like it. Olivier shifted uncomfortably, wondering what they should do, when by accident he bumped into one of the fence boards and a note — middle C — sounded loud and clear.

"I've **PITCHED** that fence **PERFECTLY**, haven't I?" Mr. Mirific bellowed. "Come in, come in. Don't be shy. I'm not! Enter my **NOT-SO-HUMBLE** home!"

Since this seemed to be one of those invitations that didn't involve much choice, Olivier and his friends shuffled in reluctantly, all a bit shamefaced at having been found out so easily.

"Well, well, **WELL**," Mr. Mirific roared, up and down the scale. "I thought you'd come around. Haw, haw!"

"Okay, so what have you done with *him*? And *it*?" demanded Linnet, mincing no words.

Unfortunately, Mr. Mirific liked his words minced, so the response she got was somewhat chopped. "Him? Who? It? What?"

"You know what I mean, Mirific."

"That's **MR.** to you. **MR. MIRIFIC!!** I'm a capital fellow."

"Stop playing games."

"You can't be serious? What an idea! A dangerous idea, don't you think?" Here he turned to Olivier and said in a stage whisper, "I'd watch *her*. Girls, you know, always spoiling the **FUN**."

Since Olivier recognized this as the old divide-and-conquer dodge, he responded, "Not true. Boys spoil an equal amount. I'd say roughly half."

Mr. Mirific gave him a shrewd look, then hopped down from the platform and stuck out his hand. "I don't believe we've met, lad. Name's Mirific, rhymes with **TERRIFIC**."

His handshake fell somewhere in the firm to electric range and Olivier wondered if he didn't have one of those joke buzzers concealed in his palm. He didn't. He had something else, which he slipped to Olivier with a wink and a waggle of his eyebrows. Caught off guard, Olivier said nothing, but casually slid his hand into his pocket, depositing the thing there for later inspection.

"Master Flood." Mr. Mirific had now turned his attention to Fathom. "I'm so glad you could drip drop in. Still wet behind the ears, I see."

Fathom smiled weakly, putting up with it.

"You know, my sprat, just say the word, *the word*,

and I will turn the course of your life around. A few minor verbal adjustments and you'll no longer have to be a Mama's boy, a mere tributary — you can be a *tribulation*! Why be nautical? How dull! When you can be *naughty* instead?"

Olivier didn't have a clue what Mr. Mirific was talking about, although Fathom must have understood, for his barely polite smile turned into a puckish grin and he had a cool considering look in his eyes, as if tempted.

"Mirific," Linnet broke the spell, "what are you blathering about?"

"That's **MISTER**, sister. Don't make me less, lass, than I am. There's **MORE** to me than meets the eye. Yes, indeed. I have ideas. I have notions. I have plans. I have *Inklings!*"

Olivier gave a start. The Inklings!

"So *you're* the one," said Linnet.

"Naturally, I'm the one. **THE ONE AND ONLY** … now that you mention it. Yes, the little devils work for me now. I keep them busy, too. A deletion here, an addition there. I'm renovating the language, you see. Improving it, modernizing it. Some of it is so old and creaky and useless — forsooth and all that. I mean, you've no idea … because *I* have them all! Yuk, yuk."

"You're the one who turned all the owls into bowls?"

"I did, I did. Much more useful, don't you think? Ever tried to eat your potato chips out of an owl?"

"*You* turned the dukes into ducks."

"Ha! Bunch of quacks."

"And the goslings into godlings!"

"A stroke of genius."

"But they're such snobs now and they won't eat properly … all they want is ambrosia."

"My dear, don't be such a peasant. I've improved their lot in life, elevated them above the swamps and murky ponds. Now they can really *be* something."

"What's wrong with being a goose?"

"*You* can be a goose if you like. I'd rather be a **G◉D**."

"You *can't* do this!" Linnet was getting huffy and puffy with exasperation and the air around her felt charged, as though a storm might break out at any moment and go crashing around the yard.

"And why not?" Mr. Mirific seemed greatly amused.

"Because it's wrong."

"Sorry, got rid of that word. It's spelled 'r-o-n-g' now and two of them make a 'r-i-t-e.'"

"The new rules," said Olivier, remembering what he had overheard at the So-Sos' campsite.

"That's *it*," squealed the little man. "My, but you're a quick study. I could use a youngster like you, someone who's **INTELLIGENT, KN◉WLEDGEABLE, HANDS◉ME,** not to mention **SUAVE, AND BRAVE**, oh yes, *very*, farseeing *and* jumping. You are a rare find, my boy, **SPECIAL, UNI◉UE!**"

Since Olivier actually was intelligent, he knew he was being sold a bill of goods. And yet, and yet … how hard it is sometimes to resist such blandishments. They went in one ear and had a bit of a struggle getting out the other, for they made a stopover in between, where he briefly savoured them, enjoying a moment of vanity.

"Think about it," urged Mr. Mirific.

Olivier didn't have much of a chance to do so, for a cool fist of air rapped him smartly on the noggin. Glancing over at Linnet, he shrugged.

"But heavens," said Mr. Mirific, "I'm forgetting myself — imagine! Do come in, come in and we'll have 'T,' or 'X,' or 'Y.' Really I have so many spares around these days. I'm getting to be so **FAMOUS**, so **BIG**, I simply must publish my letters."

"Is that what these empty books are for?" said Fathom, who had drifted off and was poking around the yard. He had come across a number of books, randomly placed here and there, open flat, pages completely blank.

"Careful, don't get watermarks on them!" shouted Mr. Mirific. "Those are the traps."

"Traps?"

"Fiendishly clever of me. You see, the Inklings can't resist a blank page and the minute one alights the book *snaps* shut and I got 'im!"

"You mean," said Linnet, "you capture them and force them to work for you?"

"Something like that." He hurled the megaphone away, then slapped his small hands together and rubbed them vigorously. "Great changes ahead. **MAGNIFICENT** changes. Seen your dictionary lately? Bet you haven't. Bet no one has, because I have them all! Or did have. Most of them had to be destroyed, *liquid*ated — *eh*, Master Flood? — put out of their misery, or perhaps I should say, the misery they were giving *me*."

"The So-So Gang," it suddenly struck Olivier. "They were burning books."

"My goodness **ME**, you should be a detective! How right you are and who would have guessed that such a hopeless pack of ninnies could be so useful? But hark, or is that *hork*? What a coincidence. There's one of them now, my very own morphew, I mean, nephew, coming through the gate. If it isn't the not-so-great and sputtering Sputum himself."

So it was. Sputum had entered the yard and bowed very low as he approached, rocking his hand in the So-So greeting. He had news to tell and not only was he already telling it, he was giving the grass a good watering besides.

"Straighten up," Mr. Mirific shouted. "No grovelling allowed. And don't expect me to return that ridiculous salute. I've never committed a mediocrity in my whole **GLORIOUS** life."

"Sire, Sir, Mister, I bear spectacular, stupendous, startling...." As Sputum screeched to a halt his wig took flight, although he managed to snag it in midair and clap it back on his head, sideways.

"Spit it out," ordered Mr. Mirific and, as if on cue, everyone took a giant step backward.

Fortunately, Sputum's news, absorbed mostly by his wig, was brief. "They are found," he announced. "We have them, *both* of them!"

"**BRAVO**, Sputum. **EXCELLENT** work! I hereby promote you to General, if that's not too vague. Where are they?"

Sputum glanced at the others.

"Never mind *them*," said Mr. Mirific, dismissively. "They're only *children*. No threat at all."

This comment did not make Mr. Mirific popular in the least. They all glared at him, Olivier as if seeing the little man clearly for the first time.

"Caught 'em in that shambles of a shack in the swamp, sir."

With a flourish Mr. Mirific pulled a huge purple handkerchief out of his sleeve and wiped his face. "I must say you're a positive *fountain* of glad tidings. Tell me, what have you done with them?"

"Got the green one planted in a pot, yer bigness. He ain't going nowhere."

"And Dirk Smith?"

"Six So-Sos is keep 'im under surveillyance. Security's shipshape, fer sure, sir."

"Dear **ME**, in that case I'd better go immediately." He turned to Linnet. "To answer your question ... what was it now? Oh yes, 'What have I done with them?' Suffice to say, you'll see. Since you'll be detained here for a spell, do make yourselves at home."

"We're not staying here," said Linnet, indignantly.

"*Au contraire*, but you *are*." Mr. Mirific snapped his fingers once, twice ... three times (a little impatiently) and an enormous dog appeared at the top of the clown slide, skidded down, nails clattering, then lumbered over to them, puffing smoke.

"Meet my moni*cur*, kiddies. This is Ashley, the fire-dog. He'll keep an eye on you, won't you, boy?"

"Wough," the dog said, a spurt of flame shooting out of his mouth as if from a lighter.

"Don't worry," Mr. Mirific said, strutting past them and through the gate, "it'll be locked."

Sputum scurried behind him, barely making it through before the gate snapped shut with a decisive *click*.

"Mirific," called Linnet, an ill wind already beginning to prowl around the yard, searching for an exit, "you're *short* and *funny-looking* and you *won't* get away with this!"

"Sour grapes, *eh*?" His voice began to fade. "Tough beans, *huh*?" They could hardly hear him. "Rotten luck, what?"

Rotten luck?

THIRTEEN
(again!)

I think he's got a cold," said Olivier.

"More like a 'hot,'" joked Fathom.

Linnet groaned. "Don't *you* start. I heard enough of that from the old punster himself."

They were all staring at Ashley, who was having a coughing fit. The air around him had grown quite hot and he kept setting things on fire. Fathom was quick to put these fires out, conjuring blasts of water like a magician, but it was hard work and the effort was literally draining him.

"Fathom, we've got to get you back to the river," Linnet said. "And then we've got to find the woodwose and Dirk before Mirific does. And we're *trapped*."

"Wough, wough," Ashley wheezed and a tongue of fire licked up Linnet's sleeve. She slapped her arm, promptly extinguishing the flames, the way you might flatten a pesky mosquito.

"I've got it," said Olivier. "I'll jump. I'll use the skip-jack to get over the fence."

"Won't work. I've already sent a wind sweep up and around. You can't see it, but there's some sort of dome above us, an invisible barrier."

"Like a force field, you mean?"

"Something like that. You'd go splat if you tried to jump through it. Mirific's got more than a few tricks up his sleeve. I wonder why he wants Dirk so badly?"

"Maybe if we found the Inklings we'd have a better idea of what this was all about. I wonder where he's hiding them," said Olivier, looking around. Then he said, "Fathom, are you okay?"

Poor Fathom *was* wavering a bit, as though he were beginning to evaporate.

"Collywobbles," he said faintly.

"Come on," urged Linnet, "we'll go into Mirific's lodge. He's got to have water in there. What you need is a good soak. Olivier, will you stay with Ashley and make sure he doesn't burn the place down?"

"Yes, of course." Funny, the firedog was supposed to be keeping an eye on them, not the other way around. "Go. Hurry."

Linnet ignored Mr. Mirific's various elevating contraptions and simply raised her arms. In doing so, she summoned a vortex of wind that picked them both up and carried them, tornado-style, to a landing above. They then passed through a door shaped like a comma.

As he watched them go, Olivier thought how very much *he'd* like to see inside Mr. Mirific's place. But at present he had his work cut out for him — Ashley was having an incendiary sneezing fit and Olivier had to jump around like a frenzied modern dancer stomping out budding fires.

Then Ashley did something even more remarkable, something Olivier had been hoping for all along. You know how you say to a dog, "Speak, boy, speak!" well, Ashley *did*. Olivier heard him muttering unhappily to himself as he plodded around the yard:

> Swallowed something indigestible
> tasted quite detestable
> it's made me most combustible
> think I'll bark a spark, or two —
> wough, wough

Olivier was so delighted that he bent down immediately to offer his sympathies. "You ate something that didn't agree with you?" He wondered if he dare give the dog a pat on the head.

"Mmmph," murmured Ashley, sounding exactly like one of Olivier's uncles after a huge Thanksgiving dinner.

Olivier reached out and ruffled his fur, which was a mistake. He pulled his hand back instantly and blew on his singed fingers — imagine ruffling hot coals. The fire-dog appreciated the friendly gesture, though, for he nodded his head, indicating that Olivier should follow him. They walked around to the side of Hodgepodge Lodge, where Olivier saw a black iron cauldron — Ashley's food dish, apparently, for his name was inscribed on it.

"Check it out," mumbled the dog, so Olivier went over to it and had a look inside, thinking to himself, *What does a firedog eat, anyway?*

"Books!" he gasped. "Oh my gosh, he makes you *eat* these?" The cauldron contained the charred remains of what looked suspiciously and alarmingly like Olivier's own personal library. He stared in disbelief at the burned covers and bindings and half-consumed volumes of *The Sword in the Stone, A Wizard of Earthsea, The Book of Three, Simon Jesse's Journey, The Phantom Tollbooth, Mrs. Frisby and the Rats of NIMH* and *The Magician's Nephew*. He felt as if someone had punched him in the stomach. These were his *friends*.

Ashley sighed deeply. A trickle of smoke coiled out of his nose and a single tear rolled down his cheek, sizzling like water on a griddle.

Olivier plucked a copy of *Treasure Island* out of the cauldron. It didn't seem as damaged as the rest, but when he opened it the pages crumbled into ashes, some of which simply drifted away.

"I hope you enjoyed it," he said, more bitterly than he meant to, knowing that it wasn't the firedog's fault.

"Preferred *Kidnapped*," Ashley moaned.

"Oh, but *Treasure Island*'s a better book."

"Found it a bit dry."

Ashley began to choke and splutter and wheeze once again.

"Symbols," he almost gagged, "hard to swallow."

"So, it's not only dictionaries Mr. Mirific is getting rid of, but really *good* books, too?"

"Blaaaa," was all Ashley had to say about that. He *was* in considerable distress.

"C'mon, boy, try to cough it up." If only Olivier could slap Ashley on the back without frying his hand. He couldn't help but be reminded of his earlier meeting with the woodwose — the creatures in this place ate the queerest things.

Suddenly, a commotion broke out. The keyboard fence started playing a raucous and zany tune, fireworks began shooting out of the lodge's many chimneys, balloons began pouring through open windows and a whole marching band of mechanical toys slid down the clown's tongue and paraded around blowing horns, thumping on drums and clashing cymbals. Then Ashley sneezed his biggest sneeze yet and sent a fireball roaring through the yard, bowling over the marching toys, popping balloons and burning a perfectly round hole the size of a softball through the locked gate.

"Yay!" shouted Olivier. Not only did the hole, however small, look like a way out — surely he could reach through and unlock the gate? — but Ashley had sneezed out his problem. The very thing he'd been choking on now lay before him on the ground, glowing red-hot.

"A *key*." Olivier crouched down for a closer look.

"Ahhhhhh," sighed Ashley grinning from ear to floppy ear.

Once the key had cooled somewhat, Olivier picked it up, a finely wrought object of gold and silver. Strange thing was, it bore a family resemblance to Dirk Smith. But why and how did Ashley come by it?

"Yours," the firedog panted.

"Mine? You want me to have it? Are you sure? I mean, it looks valuable. You didn't eat a diary, did you?"

"List." Ashley thumped his tail on the ground, sending up a spray of sparks.

"My list?" Did *everyone* here know about the scavenger hunt? "But I don't have to find a key." *On the other hand*, he thought, *maybe I do.* "Thanks, Ashley," he said.

The firedog nodded and began humming contentedly like an electric heater.

"Hey, Olivier! Did you see *that*? Wasn't it great?" It was Fathom, sliding down a peppermint pole to the ground, taking a few licks as he went. His hair was flat as a cap and dripping wet and his skin, no longer a murky colour, had the shimmery golden glow of sunlight reflected on water.

"Pretty hard not to," Olivier laughed. "I see you found some water, too."

"You bet, a whole pool."

"Up *there*?"

"Yeah, you wouldn't believe that place. It's got rooms and rooms *and* rooms. One room had a whole wall with buttons and knobs and switches on it and all I did was push and turn and pull a few of those and things really started to happen."

"I'll say. Maybe I'd better go up and have a look," Olivier suggested. "Where's Linnet?"

"Here," she called, swooping down in the airplane elevator and hopping out. "See what I found?"

As she approached, Olivier saw that she was carrying what seemed to be a miniature treasure chest.

"Listen," she said, holding it up to his ear. He heard a busy buzzy clamouring sound inside. For some reason, he immediately felt a jolt of inspiration, as though he could compose a poem or a speech right on the spot.

"What's in there?" he asked. "Sounds like bees."

"Try again."

Ah, he had an idea, then another and another after that... "Inklings!"

"Yes!" Linnet could scarcely contain herself and was hopping around in delight. "Bet Mirific didn't think I could find them, but I *did*. It wasn't that hard, actually, with some help from an undercurrent — his place *is* drafty. Why don't we set them free? That would mess up his plans."

"The chest is probably locked," said Fathom.

"Sure it is, but Olivier has a key. Where did you get it, anyway?" Linnet asked.

Olivier held up the key. "Ashley. He *talked* to me."

She raised an eyebrow and gave him a pitying look.

"He *did* speak to me. We practically had a conversation, didn't we, Ashley?"

The firedog grinned and thumped his tail, but remained mute as a stone.

Linnet only sighed and held out the chest, saying, "Here, let's see if you can open it."

Olivier tried to fit the key into the lock, but it wouldn't work.

"Darn," said Linnet. "I guess we'll have to look around for another key. Mirific probably has dozens. Which reminds me, what did he slip you earlier? The thing you put in your pocket?"

"Right, I forgot about that. How did you know?"

"Mirific can't do anything without making a show of it, even being sneaky. It was fairly obvious."

Olivier fished around in his pocket and pulled out … a stale, rock-hard jujube, a *black* one, to add insult to injury. "Great," he groaned, "and I thought it was going to be something useful."

"He wanted you to think that," said Fathom. "He was probably making fun of your scavenger hunt."

Annoyed, Olivier threw the candy straight through the hole the fireball had made in the front gate. He must have fired it with some force, too, for someone on the other side of the gate said, "Ow!" or was it, "Mee-ow?" A familiar furry face appeared at the opening and peeked in.

"Poe!" Olivier exclaimed. "Where did you come from? Are you okay? Hey, and there's Zeke, too. I wondered where you'd gotten to."

Poe didn't waste any time. She leapt through the opening and into the yard, followed closely by Zeke, who, in greeting, skimmed a noisy circuit around everyone's head. These two, however, weren't the only new arrivals for, in a small quiver strapped to Poe's side, Olivier spotted — "Murray!"

He looked to be in fine form, too, ready to roll. (Well, if he were a ballpoint he'd have rolled.) He was ready to write, in any event, which he did. He *was* a bit choked up at first, his ink somewhat clear and salty, but soon it turned a deep bold blue. *Onward, my boy,* he urged. *We have a new chapter to write, a civilization of books to save, a creature to name, heroics enough for everyone, small, medium and large, and the gate's not even locked!*

FØURTEEN

"**N**OT LOCKED?" said everyone as Linnet turned the huge knob and the gate swung open.

"NOT LOCKED!" said everyone again, except Ashley, who contributed a wheezy, "Wough, wough!" Zeke didn't seem in the least surprised.

"But he *said....*"

"Do I feel dumb."

"It doesn't matter," said Olivier. "We have the Inklings." For the benefit of newcomers to the group, he pointed to the humming treasure chest in Linnet's hands.

My, enthused Murray. *Well done*.

"Murray's right, though," continued Olivier. "We'd better get going. Fathom, why don't you lead the way? You must know how to get to this swampy place Sputum was talking about."

"Sure. C'mon, we'll take the shortcut."

As they streamed through the gate, Olivier turned to take a last look at Hodgepodge Lodge. He regretted not having a chance to explore it further. Then, seeing Ashley looking so dejected and lonely, he said, "Why don't you come with us, join the search?"

Ashley was overjoyed at this suggestion. Leaping to his feet, he fired off a volley of barks, which caused everyone to pick up speed and dash out of sight.

"You have to promise not to set fire to the woods," Olivier added.

"Got it," muttered Ashley, who charged after the rest of them.

"Did you hear that, Murray? Ashley spoke."

I'd much rather hear you talk, my boy. Bliss is still at the cottage with Sylvan, by the way, keeping an eye on things at that end. Now, tell me everything that has happened to you.

So Olivier walked and talked, tracing his own story as they followed the path deeper into the woods. He told about getting lost at night, how the cat's-eye had helped him, about the So-So Gang and how he'd been captured by the woodwose and Linnet.

"She's the one who shot you. An accident, really, a case of mistaken identity."

At this news, Murray snorted an exclamation mark of angry purple ink on Olivier's pocket. Trying to ignore the fact that he was now punctuated, Olivier went on to tell about the trek through the treetops, the river, Ma Flood and Fathom and the absurd trouble-making

Mr. Mirific. He also spoke of the other scavenger hunt objects he'd found, how he never seemed to recognize them at first and what strange, individual powers they possessed. He was so absorbed in relating all these events that at one point he stopped and said, "I wonder where the others have gotten to? We should have caught up to them by now and I can't even hear them up ahead."

I do hope it hasn't happened again, wrote Murray.

"Lost, you mean? I don't see how. We've stuck to the path and it hasn't branched off or anything."

"Dommage."

Olivier could have sworn he'd heard something, a tiny voice sighing in his ear, but when he stopped and looked around he couldn't see anyone.

What's wrong? asked Murray.

"Nothing. I thought I heard a voice. It sounded small. Far away, I guess." He heard the voice again, but this time it seemed to be scattered around his head, tiny words tossed in the air like confetti. If he gathered the words up and arranged them in a sentence he would get:

"Quel fou, perdu, dommage, dommage, fou, perdu, quelle dommage...."

"Who said that?" Once again Olivier gazed around, perplexed. All he could see was a cluster of insects dancing crazily in a drifting cloud.

Oh, them, declared Murray. *Tell them to get lost.*

"Who? You don't mean those bugs?"

Yes, of course. They're French flies.

"Murray, what a terrible pun. You're as bad as Mr. Mirific."

But that's what they're called. Ask them.

"*Oui, oui, oui, oui, non, oui, bien sûr.*"

"Gosh, it *is* them. Hey, hi there! *Bonjour!*"

The cluster now convened around his head like a shifting, speckled aura. "*Bon, bon jour, bon jour, ça va, va, va?*"

How he wished he had paid more attention in French class. "*Bien,*" I think. "*Comment vous appelez-vous?*" On second thought, maybe he shouldn't have asked them that. If they were all going to tell him their names, it could take all day. Considering that there had to be hundreds of them, their answer was unexpectedly short. "*Je, je, je, je suis, je, je suis Guy, Guy, Guy MXIV.*"

Guy MXIV, mused Murray, *an aristocratic bunch.*

"I don't get it. Which one is Guy?"

They all are.

"They're *all* Guy?

The 1014th. Right.

Olivier thought this over. "Interesting," is what he finally concluded, which is sometimes all one can conclude about unusual arrangements. " '*Perdu*' means lost, doesn't it?"

Right again.

"Shoot."

Exactly.

"But, Murray, Guy should know the way, don't you think? Bugs love swampy places. Maybe they, I mean he, can give us directions."

Our friend is a bit scatterbrained, if you ask me.
Might lead us farther astray.

"*La plume de ma tante, eh, eh, eh, hee, hee, hee.*"

Pestilence.

"Guy," Olivier began, grasping at the odd bits of French that were dancing around inside his head. "*Savez-vous le, le,* ahh, *la,* no, *le, la*...

"*Chanson? Mais oui, la la la, la la.*"

"No, no. *Le chemin,* that's it. *Le chemin que nos amis, nos amis....*"

"*Ahhhh, oui, oui, oui! Pas de problem, eh, eh, eh, eh? Venez, venez, venez.*"

Having grasped the problem and quickly infested it, Guy was soon escorting Olivier and Murray through the woods, all the while singing fragments of songs, delivering shreds of advice and *bon mots* and making minute, pin-sized points about nothing in particular. Marching along within this enveloping and chattering cloud gave new meaning to the term "French immersion."

When they finally emerged from the forest, Olivier was relieved to see the slender spikes of bulrushes ahead and smell the pungency of a marsh.

"There they are!" shouted Fathom. "I think...."

"*Voilà, voilà, voilà vos, vos, vos, vos amis, amis.*"

The flies' triumphant, if faint, announcement was followed by a compact collective gasp and a change of tune. "*Oh-oh, au, au revoir, je, je, je dois aller vite, vite aller, au revoir....*"

"Wait," pleaded Olivier. "Don't go."

But Guy had pulled himself hastily together into a tight formation and shot back into the woods.

"What happened?"

Caught sight of Zeke, I believe. He likes his snacks, you know, his petits hors-d'œuvres, eh, eh, eh.

"I guess I'd clear out, too," he laughed. "Hey, hi Linnet!"

"Olivier," she ran toward him. "Where were you?"

"You won't believe who I was talking to ... oh, never mind. Who's that?" Someone was tied to a tree that stood beside an old ramshackle lean-to.

"It's Wen, from the So-So Gang. She helped the woodwose escape and the others were so mad at her that they tied her up and were torturing her."

"How horrible! I didn't think they were that bad."

"Well, their version of torture. They were calling her names like 'Four-Eyes' and sticking gum in her hair."

"That's bearable, I guess. Still, it was brave of her to go against the whole gang. Let's set her free."

"I'll be there in a sec, but could you take the Inkling chest for a bit? I mean, I'd like to talk to Murray. I owe him an apology."

"It's up to him, I guess. Murray?"

Fine, he responded icily. *I consider her a most dangerous individual. Perhaps I will find a way of stabbing her in the hand with my nib.*

"You wouldn't do that," said Olivier.

Hah!

Quickly exchanging his friend and notebook for the Inklings, Olivier ran over to Wen. "Good plan, good plan," he could have sworn he heard them saying, like a muffled chorus of cheerleaders. Fathom was crouched behind the tree and muttering something about how Dirk Smith would have made quick work of this knotty business. By the looks of things, the So-So Gang had gotten a bit carried away. Wen was cinched like a package. She was not only tied with cord, but also with the unravelled yarn from a sweater, a vine, several shoelaces and a great length of string that was wound round and round her. Olivier introduced himself. Understandably, she couldn't shake hands, but he did congratulate her for her so un-So-So-like deed. Then, peering closely at her hair, he said, "Grape. That's *my* gum, you know. And, that's *my* string."

"Yeah," said Wen. "They frisked the woodwose for Dirk, but all they found was this stuff."

"Don't tell me he's lost Dirk?"

"Dunno. Maybe he hid it somewhere."

"What happened to Mr. Mirific and the others?"

"They ran off that way," she indicated the far end of the swamp by pointing her nose in a northerly direction. "Say, would you mind?"

"Not at all." Olivier placed his index finger on the bridge of her glasses, where the masking tape was, and pushed up. "There."

"Thanks. The woodwose didn't go with them, though. He ran into the shed."

"He did?" Olivier was surprised that anyone could even go near the tottery old building without knocking the thing down, especially someone the size of the woodwose. It really did look shaky, built as it was out of rotten boards, driftwood, sticks and a few odd shingles, with moss for the roof.

"Yup. Disappeared. Don't ask me how. When I broke the pot they'd planted him in — gosh, he was starting to root — he dashed straight in there and didn't come out. Craven and Fuss ran in after him and they disappeared too. The rest of the gang was in a lather, as usual, running all over the place and bumping into one another, so that nobody else saw the three of them go inside. I refused to talk, so they tied me up. When Mirific and Sputum came along, I pretended I was scared of them, told them that the woodwose and the other two had run away. That sent them off in the wrong direction. I figure they'll be back when they don't find them. And soon."

"Great work. How are those knots coming, Fathom? We've got to get out of here."

"Can't seem to get 'em."

"I know. Ashley, c'mere boy."

"Wough," said the firedog, ambling over with a smile on his chops. He had just managed to roast a minnow for Poe, a delicate culinary operation of which he was quite proud.

"Can you burn through these?" Olivier showed him where Wen's bonds were most thickly knotted. "Without burning Wen, that is?"

Ashley gave a knowing and confident nod and set to work.

Poe and Zeke came over to watch and Linnet and Murray soon joined them.

Splendid girl, Murray confided.

Olivier smiled, pleased that they'd made amends, then stooped down to pick up something that had caught his eye, something flashing golden in the grass. A coin. "Look at this. It's got a nose embossed on one side — a real honker — and some writing on the other: *Non possumus.* I wonder what that means?"

Good grief, you mean to tell me they don't teach young people Latin any more? Incredible! When I think of the declensions I penned in my youth. It means "We cannot." And with a motto like that it could only be So-So currency. I expect that it's of no value whatsoever. Not worth a doit.

"A doit? A *doit,* Murray?"

Ahh, yes. I see.

"Everyone, Wen's free!" said Fathom. "Three cheers for Ashley."

But before Ashley's success could be properly celebrated, or the coin further examined, Linnet interrupted with, "Shh, listen. Someone's coming."

"It's *them,*" said Wen, rubbing her arms and shaking the circulation back into her fingers. "Quick, into the shed."

Without giving it another thought — such as, *Was this a good idea?* or *Would they even fit?* — they all rushed in, one after another, and promptly disappeared.

FIFTEEN

One thing was certain, the inside of the shed was much larger than the outside. The moment they entered, they found themselves in a maze of rough reedy walls. They stumbled and groped their way along in the dark — going first in one direction, then in another, arriving at dead ends, doubling back, turning sharp corners, travelling if not in circles, then definitely in squares.

"Olivier, can't you *do* something?" Linnet asked, exasperated. "Maybe the sunstone will help us find our way out of here. I don't like this."

"Me neither." For some reason, Olivier was having difficulty breathing. And since this was a labyrinth, he couldn't help but think of minotaurs. (And thanks to the So-So Gang he didn't even have his string ball handy.) Nor could he figure out how this entire maze could possibly fit inside the shed. He was going to have to try *something*.

(Murray, meanwhile, was musing about how much this walk through the maze resembled scribbling and made about as much sense. He was also contemplating how dry his comments were going to get if he didn't soon knock back a cartridge or two.)

Still gripping the doit in one hand, Olivier reached into his pocket with the other and pulled out the sunstone. He held it out before him like a flashlight and slowly it began to glow. Then it winked once, twice … and flickered out.

"Battery's dead," observed Wen.

"That's not how it works," Olivier explained, not that he knew how it *did* work. "I wonder if I've used up its power already. Might only be good for one go. Or, maybe we don't really need it to find the way. That's a possibility."

If it weren't so dark, Olivier might have noticed that everyone was looking at him strangely, not because of what he said, but because of how he said it.

"Why are you speaking like that?" asked Fathom.

"Wough," agreed Ashley.

"Like what?"

"Sounds like you've got a clothespin on your nose," said Wen.

That was a bit much, he thought, coming from a So-So. But then he realized that his voice did sound odd — nasally and twangy, like a country and western singer. "Must be allergies," he said. "I suppose we're stirring up a lot of dust. Hey, that tickles." Raising his hand to his face, he saw Zeke was doing a dragonfly dance on the back of it, dipping and bobbing, moving his black thread-like legs so energetically that Olivier wanted to laugh. Instead, he sneezed, so hard that he blew Zeke away, far down the corridor. The doit flew out of his hand.

"Gosh, I didn't mean to do that, Zeke," Olivier called after him. "But I do feel a lot better, I can breathe again."

"The doit," said Fathom. "It has a nose on it, right? I bet you were holding it too tight and that's why you sounded different, like you were pinching your own nose. Zeke was trying to help by tickling you."

"That's kooky," said Wen.

"No wait, Fathom's got it. The doit must have something to do with breathing, or sniffing things out, like a bloodhound."

"A second nose? Great!" said Linnet. "Maybe you can catch a cold with it."

Olivier immediately got down on his hands and knees and groped around for the doit. Once he had it back in his hand, he held it more carefully than before, making sure he didn't squeeze it. Then he took a deep breath — testing, testing — and exhaled slowly. "I can smell *everything*," he said. "It's incredible."

"*Ick*," said Linnet.

"In this place?" asked Wen. "All I can smell is the dampness. Wet clay, or something."

"No, no, there's much more than that here. Earthworm

and loam, sassafras root, a touch of toad, a hint of bladderwort, dead shrew, burned oak (Ashley drooling smoke), lichen, mushrooms, pepperoni and bacon."

"Wait a minute," said Linnet. "That can't be right."

"It is, though. Definitely." And his stomach growled in support.

"Okay, let's follow it," said Fathom. "A food smell has got to take us somewhere."

"We'll have to backtrack. I don't think I'll be able to smell it much longer if we keep going the way we're headed."

"I had an inkling we were going the wrong way." A muted cheer resounded in the chest Linnet was carrying. "Several of them, really," she laughed. "Come on, Olivier," her scepticism gone, "put your best nose forward and trace that scent."

As it turned out, a second snoot wasn't such a bad thing to have after all and Olivier used his well, leading them back through the maze and down passages they wouldn't have found otherwise. Eventually, it led them to a doorway where the fragrance was so strong that everyone, and not just Olivier, could smell it.

"This is it," said Linnet. "Go ahead, Olivier. Knock."

"Why me? I got us here. You knock."

The door had some alarming features. It was massive, for one thing, at least three times their size, and was made of thick, rough wooden planks that were studded with iron bolts. In addition, it had a number of lances, broadswords and a morgenstern sticking into it. All told, it seemed more like the kind of door one might encounter on the way to a dungeon, or to a monster's lair, than on the way to lunch.

"Might not be pepperoni, after all," ventured Wen.

"We could turn back," said Fathom.

"And try to get through the maze again? Not likely," said Linnet.

"This is odd." Olivier said, pointing to the doorbell. "Look, it's so ordinary, with a little light and everything, exactly like the kind you might find on a house on my street. Should I press it?"

"Go ahead."

When Olivier placed his finger on the button and pushed, they heard the bell ring pleasantly within — *ding dong* — followed, however, by what seemed like an embarrassed pause, then a kind of doorbellish throat-clearing and a whole series of horrible cries, groans and shrieks, topped off with the shrill scream of someone falling off a cliff.

I believe it's ham you've been smelling, my boy. Murray, drafted back into action, might have had a steadying effect on Olivier's nerves if there hadn't been worse to follow.

The occupant of the room behind the door had been roused and now they heard a furious roaring within and the sound of footsteps, heavy crashing footsteps, approaching. They all stood quaking, too terrified to run, bracing themselves as the door swung slowly open. There, standing in the doorway facing them, was not exactly a monster, but a creature of equal disrepute — a teenager. Yes, that's what it was, complete with a sneer on his lips, spots on his face, a buzz cut and a slab of pizza in his hand. Everyone groaned with a mixture of relief and disappointment.

"Oh, it's *you* lot," the teenager said, his sneer quickly changing into a grin. "I thought it was somebody selling something. You know how it is, seems like we're under siege here sometimes," he indicated the weaponry stuck in the door. "That's why we rigged up the maze and the taped screams and whatnot. Did it work? Were you scared out of your wits? You shoulda come to the front door. There, we've got a doormat that screams when you step on it. So, like, it's Linnet and Fathom, eh? Who are your friends? Wait a sec, come on in and meet the others, introductions all round. You like pepperoni on your pizza, or what?" Still chattering away, the teenager turned on the heel of his platform boots and beckoned them to follow.

Actually I prefer blotting paper on mine. Who is this zitty individual?

"Yeah," echoed Olivier. "You *know* him, Linnet?"

"Sure, that's Moley," she said. "He's a Wise Guy, one of the Two Holies I told you about earlier."

"Him? A *wise* guy?"

"Loosely speaking. They're a brother-and-sister team — Holy Moley and Holy Hannah. The 'wise' in their job description used to have quotation marks around it, so it was more ironic, you see. Some Inklings apparently stole them." Here, a noise that sounded suspiciously like snickering erupted from the treasure chest. "And now they really do have to be wise. They try anyway."

What next?

If Olivier could have guessed what *was* next, he might not have crossed that threshold so readily.

SIXTEEN

"I have to do *what*?" Olivier said, practically choking on his fourth slice of pizza.

The whole crew was sprawled comfortably on the floor, on toss pillows and beanbag chairs, in Moley and Hannah's rec room. (A most unremarkable room it was, too.) The Two Holies had somehow managed to serve custom-made pizzas — tomato-red ink on Murray's, hot coals on Ashley's, mosquitoes on Zeke's. Everyone was quite content, even those accidental renegades, Fuss and Craven — no toppings on theirs — *and* the woodwose, who had a lovely heap of mulch on his. He had been so frightened when everyone first arrived, and especially worried about what Linnet was going to say to him, that he'd tried to disguise himself as a coffee table.

"There you *are*," Linnet had said, removing the

bowling trophy and the mermaid souvenir from Atlantis that Fuss and Craven had placed on top of him. "Come, woodwose, sit up. I'm not angry with you."

"You're not?"

"Of course not. Though things *would* have been a lot easier if you hadn't run off with the cats and Dirk."

"I forgot myself," he said, miserably.

"But," she continued, "we're all together now, *all* of us, aren't we?"

The woodwose may have been green, but he wasn't slow. He picked up Linnet's meaning at once and, sinking his fingers into his mass of chestnut curls, he pulled and tugged and then yanked the little dagger — Dirk Smith — right out. As he held it up, a pinecone skewered on its sharp tip like a foil, everyone hooted and cheered, which caused him to blush a bright chartreuse.

It wasn't too long after this, with Dirk buried up to his hilt in deep-dish pizza, that Hannah remarked casually to Olivier that she hoped he liked water.

"Yes, thanks," he answered, even though he'd much prefer pop. "Water will be fine."

"Not to drink," said Moley. "To swim in."

Besides looking very much like twins, the Two Holies tended to speak in a twinned manner as well. They reminded Murray of a desk set he once knew.

"Swimming?" asked Olivier. "Yeah, it's okay."

"If the dog paddle counts," murmured Linnet.

"Good," said Hannah. "Then everything should go smoothly."

"Everything?"

"You see," said Moley, "you have to swim to the bottom of Nevermore Lake."

And *this* is when Olivier said, "I have to do *what*?"

"He'll make a name for himself," sighed the wood-wose.

"I'm afraid we don't know how deep it is, or how far you'll have to go," said Hannah. "No one has ever dared go down there before."

"We're not even sure what you have to do when you get there," added Moley.

"Then why does he have to go at all?" said Wen. "Sounds dumb to me."

Olivier nodded at Wen appreciatively. The truth was he hated putting his head underwater. His parents had been after him for years to do it — swimming lessons, trips to the beach. He could hear his father saying, "Look, son, it's easy. All your friends can do it, even Horace Speechly." Yeah, well, that's because he fell in, headfirst. No possible way. Olivier figured he had a good head on his shoulders, good and dry, and that's how he planned to keep it.

"If he doesn't do it," started Hannah…

"… we won't be able to stop Mr. Mirific," finished Moley.

"What's *he* got to do with it?" asked Linnet.

"We're not sure, but there's something down there he wants to get his hands on."

"It has something to do with his big plan."

"And Dirk Smith is part of it, too."

"Somehow."

"Wait a minute," said Olivier. "This is about as clear as mud. I'm not convinced I *have* to do it, either. You two have been great and I enjoyed the lunch, but I'm not going to jump in the lake because you tell me to."

"Oh, it's not our idea, is it, Hannah?"

"No, it's hers. She wants you to do it."

"Yup, called on the Oracle Phone, direct line, said you were the one for the job."

Everyone naturally wanted to know who "she" was and what this "Oracle Phone" was and so by way of explanation the Two Holies ushered them all upstairs along a winding spiral staircase and into a high tower. This was their office and, unlike the rec room, it had proper wizardly ambience. It was well stocked with magical props and paraphernalia — shelves full of baubles, wands, rings, golden bowls of silver dust, gnarled staffs, cloaks patterned with stars and crescent moons, pointy hats, ancient texts, illuminated books with runic scripts (signed by their authors in invisible ink), crystal balls and lava lamps. There also happened to be a telephone made completely of bones, of odd sizes, all stuck together. It reminded Olivier of the time he boiled a chicken carcass and built a dinosaur out of the remains for a science project. He knew it was a phone because the thing started ringing the moment they stepped into the room.

"It's for you," said Hannah to Olivier.

"Go ahead, answer it," added Moley.

"How?" he asked.

"Pick up the tibia and say hello," responded Hannah, with a hint of impatience.

"This is ridiculous." Olivier picked up one of the bones as directed and spoke into what he hoped was the right end. "Hello," he said, tentatively.

"Darling," drawled a familiar voice on the other end. "You really must do this underwater thing, there's no time to waste. That peculiar little man, what *is* his name — Mr. Fantastic? — he's hot on your trail."

"Step-step-stepgramma? Is that *you*?"

"No, no, no, dear. I'm the Oracle, *pu-lease*. I do know her. Sylvia de Whosit of Whatsit? Brilliant woman."

It *was* her, he was positive.

"Are you having fun? How is Poe?"

"Yes, loads. And Poe is fine. I ... don't want to do this. I'm not a great swimmer and I don't like putting my head underwater."

"The best way to deal with fear is head-on — or under — I always say."

"I'm *not* afraid."

"Wonderful, because everyone is depending on you to do this. Take my word for it and remember it's extremely important to a certain individual."

Gramps?

"Now listen, somewhere in that submerged old forest is a sunken ship. In the ship's cabin you'll find what we need. Bring it back with you."

More scavenger hunting! Frankly, he was getting a little tired of this game.

"Have you found all the objects on the list?"

It *had* to be her. Who else could read his mind the way she could? Except maybe Sylvan. "No, not yet."

"Tsk, tsk. You had better hurry, you'll need them."

"How can I find them now? And what for, anyway?"

"Heavens, I can't tell you everything. Oracles are supposed to be mysterious, delivering cryptic messages and all that. I have a certain style to maintain here. So toodle-oo, good luck. Try not to get eaten."

"Don't hang up yet!"

She did, and not with a sharp *click*, but with a sound that was more like someone cracking knuckles.

"Well?" said Hannah and Moley in unison.

"I guess I'm going for a swim. Who's coming with me?"

The room fell silent. Not a single person volunteered.

"Fathom, surely you'll come?"

"I'd like to, Olivier, honest, but Ma won't let me. Nevermore Lake is strictly out of bounds. Sorry."

"Linnet?"

"No, thanks," she said with a shudder that everyone felt, a chill finger of wind running up their spines.

Olivier knew there was no point asking Poe, or Ashley, or Zeke, or even Wen. At least he had one friend who wouldn't back out on him. "I can count on you, eh, Murray?"

You can count with me, my boy, but as for going into that lake, let's just say I'm not a Waterman, or even a nosy Parker. Ha, ha.

"Very funny."

"Doesn't matter what happens to me," the wood-wose spoke up. "I'll go."

"That's very brave of you, but I'm beginning to get the idea that I'm supposed to go alone."

"That's it! Right on!" rose from the chest of Inklings, which Linnet still carried.

The woodwose now held out Dirk, offering it to Olivier.

"At least you can take the dagger with you," said Wen.

A "boo nah, boo hiss" erupted from the Inklings.

"Bad idea, I guess." Olivier stared at the chest.

"You have to, it's your only protection."

"You *do* have the scavenger hunt objects," said Linnet. "Maybe now you'll find out what the blood is for."

"I don't have them all, though, and the Oracle said I'd need every one of them."

"What do you still have to find?" asked Moley.

"Let's see." Olivier began to empty his pockets, placing the objects before him on a bench while everyone crowded around. One after another he pulled them out — sunstone, skipjack, blood, brain coral, doit. He also produced the key Ashley had coughed up and the doily.

"Spider web," said the woodwose, reaching down to trace the doily's lacy pattern. "Pretty."

"Do you think so?" asked Olivier, struck. "I mean, do you think this is the 'web' on the list?"

"*This* is your web," said Hannah, pointing to the bit on the key. "That's what this part is called, a web. *Hey*, it looks like some sort of face in profile."

"Okay, it's got to be one or the other," said Linnet.

"Take both and you'll find out which one you'll need when the time comes — doily or key. What's that leave, then?"

"Armlet and hagoday."

"Hold on a sec," said Moley, walking over to a tall cupboard and pulling a large sack out of the bottom drawer. "I meant to throw this junk out ages ago." He dragged the sack over and dumped its contents on the floor.

"Holy Moley!" said Fuss, forgetting his manners. Before them lay a mass of priceless treasure — golden crowns, chains, goblets, heavily jewelled necklaces and rings, silver helmets and chain mail — all tangled together in a glittering heap.

"You were going to throw this *out*?" asked Wen, astonished.

"Yeah," sighed Hannah. "Amazing how it piles up. We get a lot of free samples and whatnot, being Wise Guys."

"Here it is," said Moley, extracting a dull, gunmetal grey band from the pile and untangling it from a beautiful pearl necklace, which he tossed aside. He handed the band to Olivier. "Try it on. Could be the one."

"Could be." Olivier slipped it on his arm and he knew instantly that he had been given the second last object on his list. "Thanks," he said. "This is it. That just leaves the hagoday."

"Can't help you there," said Hannah.

"Didn't we used to have one of those knocking around here somewhere?"

"Stolen. Right off the door. Don't you remember?"

"What use would a door knocker be, anyway?" said Linnet. "Something that heavy would take you straight to the bottom. You're better off without it."

She's right, Olivier. Time is wasting. Better plunge in.

He began refilling his pockets. "How am I supposed to do this without any diving equipment? Not that I'd know how to use it, anyway."

"Hey, no problem," said Moley. "We can fix you up, eh, Hannah?

"Sure thing," and she whipped out of her pocket a thin, pointed wand that looked very much like a Japanese chopstick. This she smacked in her hand a couple of times, like a teacher with a pointer, and said, "Okay, what'll it be?"

"Pike?" asked Moley. "Eel? How about pond slime?"

"Pardon?" said Olivier, completely puzzled.

SEVENTEEN

Who would have thought that Hannah could perform real magic? And with something that looked like a chopstick, no less? One minute Olivier was standing in the Two Holies' office and the next he was standing completely alone on the shore of a dark and forbidding lake. *Of what use is magic*, he thought irritably, *if it can't conjure up an oxygen tank and a decent pair of flippers?* Instead, Hannah had decked him out in a variety of fins, scales, gills and spines that, put together in an orderly way, might have made a convincing fish, more or less. As it was, he felt like a gaudy marine collage. He would likely get snagged in the first bunch of waterweeds he tried to swim through.

Jump! he could hear his father say. Come on, Olivier, you can do it.

Non possumus.

Hang on, he thought, the doit! If he held onto it tightly and jumped in, that would be like holding his nose underwater, wouldn't it? With the doit he might be able to hold his breath for a very long time — but would that be long enough to reach the sunken ship and find what he had to find? He knew he was supposed to use the objects for this quest, but *how*? Say he used the brain coral to "see" where the ship was located, the skipjack to jump to that exact spot, the doit to dive down to it, the sunstone for light and navigation ... oh brother, he'd have to be a juggler to manage all that.

As Olivier shook his head in frustration, he felt something on his shoulders, lolling at his back — a hood of some sort. Reaching round, he felt another head, sleek and smooth, strange as that of an eel. He pulled this forward, slipping it over his own head, and immediately understood that there was more to this than just dress-up. He felt himself encased in another being and with this came a different way of seeing. The lake was suddenly very appealing, enticing even. He couldn't wait any longer — he *had* to jump in. He did so pronto, making a big, glorious *splash*.

Once in, Olivier was amazed to find that he loved the water, that he was an excellent swimmer and that breathing was no problem. As he used his new sporty fins to propel himself into the murky depths of the lake, he couldn't help but wonder why he'd ever spent so much time above the waterline.

The lake was a fascinating place, if somewhat

spooky. There were no bulrushes or hornworts, no schools of small fry, no scuttling crabs or crayfish. The lake was very still and very empty, haunted it seemed, although by what, Olivier couldn't imagine. He wished he'd brought Dirk Smith along, after all. He suddenly wondered if all of the Inklings' ideas were *good* ones? What if they had been under Mr. Mirific's treacherous thumb too long to give honest advice?

The deeper he swam, the darker it got. He didn't have a clue where he was going. He retrieved the sunstone and clenched it between his teeth in order to swim properly. This would work well as long as he didn't swallow it *and* if the sunstone itself didn't flicker out. As if to put his fears to rest, the sunstone instantly lit up and cast a strong searching light into the black water. It began to tug him forward, too, almost as if he were hooked and being reeled in.

Olivier swam, gliding like a stingray over rock piles and shoals and a great heap of bones. What was *that*? He couldn't stop to investigate for the sunstone kept pulling him forward, its luminous ray probing nervously this way and that. Soon, long-dead tree branches, algae-bearded and furred, began to leap at him out of the dark. He had arrived at the old forest, which quickly grew more dense and difficult to navigate. As he darted in and around the branches, he knew how Linnet must feel sometimes, like the very wind whistling through the trees.

Finally, the sunstone stopped. He steadied himself on a branch by grabbing at a frayed and rotting rope that was dangling down from above. He removed the sunstone from between his teeth and looked up. What he saw startled him so much that he almost dropped the stone. The *woodwose* peered down at him through the gloom! He swam upward, half pulling himself with the rope, and saw that the staring face was actually a carving, and a remarkable likeness of the woodwose. It was a figurehead ... he'd found the ship! Here was another boat stuck in the trees, although this one was old, like a ship from the Spanish Armada, and lodged in an underwater forest. He hoisted himself up and swam onto the deck.

Getting into the ship's cabin was going to be difficult, for the door was completely blocked by a fence of fallen branches. There wasn't enough space for Olivier to wriggle in between them and they were too thick to break off. That's what he assumed anyway, until he grabbed one of the branches and it snapped like a twig, making a muted underwater *thug*. Great luck; they were rotten. When he grabbed one with his other hand, however, he couldn't budge it. Olivier switched hands again and the branch broke easily. Ahh, yes ... the arm-let. He hadn't taken it off after first trying it on in the Wise Guys' office. So, it gave him superior strength — in one arm, anyway. Terrific! Feeling invigorated, he went to work with a passion, hurling branches away as he blazed a trail to the cabin door. I yam what I yam, he chuckled to himself, imagining what fun it would be to wield Popeye's power at home, to lift the house, say, so that his dad could vacuum under it, or to bring the whole fridge when his mum asked him to fetch her a snack.

Before long Olivier was standing in front of the cleared cabin door, reaching for the knob. Of all the doorknobs he had encountered lately, this one was the most peculiar. Creepy, even. It was shaped like a fist — a clenched human hand — and when he touched it he recoiled, for it *felt* human, too. Like skin. He clasped the knob firmly and tried to turn it, but the knob wouldn't budge. In fact, it seemed to resist. He tried again, this time using his super-strong hand, but the knob only clenched itself tighter. What to do? He didn't want to stand here wrestling with a doorknob.

Olivier almost jumped out of his fish suit when the knob suddenly unfurled its fingers and held its palm flat out, as if demanding a tip. He gaped at it, wondering what it could want. Then he began to rummage in his pockets, knowing that the only coin he had on him was the doit and he didn't want to give that away — his life might depend on it. The hand motioned impatiently, as if to say, "Come on, come on, cough it up."

All right, sighed Olivier, maybe this was what the doit was for. He found the coin and placed it smack in the knob's open palm. The hand judged the doit's weight, fingered it, then flipped it back, presenting its open palm once again. What *did* it want? He tried the key next — doors like keys, don't they? But it waved it away disdainfully. Okay, how about this? He plonked down his most puzzling scavenger hunt item — the blood. The doorknob rolled the marble round and round, gripped it lightly, held it appreciatively in the tips of its fingers as one would a precious object, then indicated that Olivier should take it back. This time it held up its thumb and index finger in an A-OK gesture and offered itself in a handshake. (It had a firm, business-like grip.) The doorknob then motioned Olivier to step forward. As he did, it gave its wrist a neat little twist and the door swung open.

The cabin he stepped into was small, but packed full of all sorts of interesting things — tankards, charts, an astrolabe, a ship's log — but for once this made his heart sink. He had hoped the "it" he was supposed to find would be obvious, that he could make a quick grab for it and be gone. Oddly, the cabin reminded him of a room that he and Murray had explored in Cat's Eye Corner. It was indeed *so* familiar he had the feeling that if he opened the little door at the other end of the cabin he would find himself looking out into the upstairs hall. He moved toward the door now, thinking it wouldn't hurt just to see, to open it a crack and satisfy his curiosity. He was on the verge of trying it when he noticed water swirling around his ankles. The cabin had been sealed when he'd entered and he hadn't even realized that he was breathing air again, but now water from outside was pouring in. He had to act *fast*.

Where was it? *What* was it? *Right*, he thought, fishing in his pocket for the brain coral. He closed his eyes, clasped it firmly in hand and a picture flashed into his mind of the thing he was supposed to find. It was a *book*. He should have guessed it would be something like that. It made perfect sense given Mr. Mirific's mission, his dictionary dictatorship, the way he was clear-cutting through the classics. But this book, the one he saw in his mind's eye, was the most ragged, ripped, down-on-its-luck volume he'd ever seen. Who would want it?

Olivier hastily scanned the cabin once more. Up there! He spotted the book tucked away on a topmost shelf. Any moment he would be able to swim toward it, for the water had risen to his neck. He would have reached the book, too, if he hadn't glanced down and seen a shadowy form in the water gliding toward him — huge and black and closing in on him in ever-tightening circles.

EIGHTEEN

Pulled under, Olivier tumbled into a terrifying darkness, one that was frisking him for his life, plucking at his eyes, plugging up his nostrils, sucking the breath right out of him. Whatever the thing was, it was shapeless and horrible. He felt as if he was being attacked by a living blanket, protean and smothering. Olivier kicked and thrashed and fought the thing until he broke free of it, gasping for air. He clung to the top shelf, inches from where the book lay. Desperately, he reached out for it, thinking that if he could just nab it and fight the creature off until he reached the cabin door, he might be able to escape.

No such luck. Before Olivier could get his hands on the book, he was dragged back under, whirled and tossed around as if he'd been dumped in a washing machine. Cheeks bulging, lungs bursting, he clawed his way up the wall. The room was almost completely underwater now, but he managed to surface into the one corner of air that remained. He clung to a submerged shelf bracket with one hand, while struggling to get at the doit with the other. It was his only hope. But he couldn't get to it before the creature surged toward him again and flattened him against the wall, knocking the last bit of breath right out of him.

This was *too much*! The attack did not inspire panic or fear, but indignation — a healthy dose of it. Olivier felt as if he'd been bodychecked by a wet sock and he thought, *I don't have to put up with this.* He struck out at the thing with his super-strong arm.

Thwup! His fist sank into a mass of what seemed very much like sodden lint. He watched in disbelief as his attacker broke up into fragments and drifting swaths, scattered into countless bits, then came back together and re-formed, even larger, more monstrous.

He wasn't exactly sure *what* it was, but it helped to picture it as nothing more terrifying than what might come rolling out from under his bed (only much larger and with bad intentions) — something made of toenail clippings and snags of thread, dried bologna rind, maybe a missing button stuck in its forehead like a Cyclopean eye — all in all, pretty hard to take seriously.

"Right," Olivier said decisively, "I know how to fix you." He didn't really, but it was worth a try. He delved into his pocket and with a soggy flourish produced the doily, which he waved menacingly at the beast. "Go on," he said. "Get out of here!"

The creature immediately backed off.

"Aha!"

Who would have thought a doily could strike fear into the heart of anything, but the creature was actually quivering, moulting motes and specks. It was growing smaller, too, compacting itself, as if to reduce its visibility. It started to slink away, creeping slowly toward the cabin door. Then, in a frantic dash, it swept through it, as if pursued by a whole *battalion* of doilies.

Not a moment too soon, either. The cabin was now completely underwater and Olivier had no choice but to try the doit. Holding his breath while quelling his rising panic, he pinched the coin tightly. It *worked*. At least, he got the sense that he'd purchased a doit's worth of time, enough, he hoped, to swim to the surface. Grabbing the book off the shelf, he swam swiftly through the door and straight up, handicapped by this new burden, but feet and fins and everything else motoring like mad. Olivier broke the surface of that brooding ink-black lake with a shout of triumph. He'd made it!

There wasn't going to be any time to celebrate, though, not a private moment to examine that ragged old book or even strip off his fish suit. Wading to shore, he became aware of a commotion at the far end of the lake. He could hear a noise, a muffled din, and in the distance saw people involved in a skirmish. It had to be Mr. Mirific and the So-So Gang battling it out with his friends. Olivier reached for the one scavenger hunt object he hadn't used while underwater — the skipjack.

Sputum and a few other So-Sos were the first to spot Olivier, although they didn't know who or even *what* he was, bounding along the shoreline like a huge sand flea and laughing aloud. (It was great fun.) He *was* very oddly dressed — terrifying to those watching him get closer and closer.

One of the gang fell to the ground as if struck, crying out, "The pain, the pain!" Most of the others, including Sputum, fled, screaming, into the nearest stand of trees.

"Come back, you lily-livered, whey-faced, bandy-legged poltroons," shouted Mr. Mirific. "It's only that *boy*." No one did, naturally. Who would?

But when Olivier landed in their midst with his final great leap from the shoreline, all his pals crowded around, including Sylvan and Bliss, who had arrived in his absence. Everyone began asking questions at once.

"What happened down there?"

"Why do you have gills on your shoulders?"

"Wough, wough?"

"Did you find it?'

"Now's no time to be reading a book, is it?"

Good questions, every one of them, and Olivier did his best to answer, telling as much as he could about his adventure, while keeping an eye on Mr. Mirific. Having been largely abandoned by his troops, the little man stood off to the side of their group, rocking on his heels, studying his fingernails, whistling a tuneless tune and pretending not to listen, meanwhile taking in every word (and no doubt thinking about how to change them). When Olivier finished his story, Murray then gave an account, in shorthand, of what had happened while he was gone.

"So it's his nibs," jeered Mr. Mirific. "Why don't you dry up, eh? Skip it, huh?"

I'll have you know a Sheaffer does not leak, blot, blubber or skip!

"Ignore him," said Sylvan, knowing this to be the most galling thing one could say to Mr. Mirific, and picked up the story where Murray had left off. (Actually, he picked up the whole thing, as no one could understand shorthand, except Sylvan.) He told Olivier how, after Mr. Mirific and the So-So Gang found their way through the maze, they broke into Hannah and Moley's place, upsetting a giant Scrabble game they had been playing, and then began calling everyone names.

"Not me," lamented the woodwose.

Everything then got thrown into confusion, Sylvan explained, because Sputum grabbed the Inkling chest and ran out the front door with it, and Mr. Mirific snatched up Dirk Smith and everybody ran after him, and a lot of So-Sos seemed to be thrubbing each other with their wooden swords, and Hannah was zapping things with a chopstick, and Ashley coughed up more smoke than a cannon.

"So who has what?" asked Olivier. "Where are the Inklings?"

"Mew, mew," replied Poe, sitting on top of the Inklings' chest. Inside, they were buzzing and muttering about not being very palatable ideas. Sputum had apparently dropped the chest when Hannah had threatened to turn him into a sprinkler. But who had Dirk?

"Here," said Moley and the dagger flashed in his hand. "Doesn't belong to me, though."

"You got that right, Pizza Face," growled Mr. Mirific, making a lunge for it.

"Back off," said Hannah, raising her chopstick in warning. "It doesn't belong to you, either."

"Why do you want it so badly, anyway?" asked Fathom. "I mean, we all used to play with it, everybody got a turn."

"Because I found out something *about* it, you little drip."

"He's bigger than *you* are," said Linnet. "And not half as wet. So *what* did you find out?"

"Well, Miss Smarty-pants, whoever has possession of Dirk has the power to be the **ABSOLUTE BEST** at everything. None of this middling, wishy-washy, do-what-you-can-dear stuff. But **BRILLIANCE, EXCELLENCE, SUPERLATIVE PERFORMANCE!!!**"

"You mean that owning Dirk is like having a Midas touch? You can turn yourself into a big shot because everything you touch turns into 'gold'?" asked Olivier.

"That's it, you can **DO ANYTHING, BE ANYTHING**."

"You can change the language? Rewrite the books?"

"Yeah, and make 'em all about **ME**, using **MY** spelling and **MY** definitions." Mr. Mirific paused, eyes aglow, fixing his gaze on Olivier. "But I need that blasted book you found. You gotta use 'em together somehow. Must be the instruction manual. So hand it over, kid."

"Keep your socks on there, Carrot Top," said Moley. "You've got the wrong Smith, man."

"What?"

"That's right," said Hannah. "That prophesy or prediction or whatever you're talking about applies to Lance Smith, not Dirk. Could even be Spike Smith, but it's definitely not Dirk."

"WHAT?"

"*We* are the Wise Guys here and *we* happen to know that Dirk belongs to the woodwose. Here you go, my friend," said Moley, handing the dagger to him.

"You must have known," added Hannah, "and that's why it troubled you so much, but also why you kept ending up with it."

If the woodwose had turned a delighted shade of green, Mr. Mirific, in contrast, had gone red as a rocket and was spluttering so much it looked as if he might blast off and zoom around the treetops.

"I don't know about any prediction," said Olivier, "but I have the feeling that the book and the dagger somehow *do* go together. So here," and he gave the book to the woodwose as well.

"For me?" the woodwose asked wonderingly, gazing at the old tattered volume.

"It's got a lock on it," said Wen. "Could be a diary."

"It'll be rusted shut," said Fathom.

The woodwose then put his eye to the keyhole. He dropped the book instantly, exclaiming, "Someone's inside, someone's in there!"

"Saphead," fumed Mr. Mirific, who had not taken off after all.

"I know who you saw," said Olivier, kindly. "Yourself."

"Me?"

"I bet there's a mirror in that lock," Olivier said. "Let's just call that an educated guess. And my second guess is that this key, the one Ashley gave me, is going to break the mirror and open the book."

When Olivier held up the key for everyone to see, Hannah said, "Hey, that profile on the web, it's the woodwose."

"Go ahead," urged Moley, "try it."

"Good thing I'm not superstitious," said Olivier, kneeling down to where the book lay. Everyone heard a tinkle of breaking glass as he inserted the key and watched with great anticipation as he turned it. Looking up at the woodwose, he said, smiling, "I think you should be the one to open it."

The woodwose bent down and with trembling hands carefully lifted open the front cover of the book. On doing so, he made the most remarkable discovery of his life — his name.

NINETEEN

"Master Timothy Tamarack Reed Bilberry Greenleaf de Grassy," the woodwose read out haltingly. "That's me," he said. He had a very strange look on his face, as if something long forgotten, buried deep in memory, had sprouted anew.

"You?" said Olivier. "This is *your* name? You've found it!"

Drat, scribbled Murray, *and I was just about to suggest that one.*

"You're the little sprig on this family tree," said Sylvan, pointing to the flyleaf of the book. "It's an important family, too, by the sounds of it. Lady Dittany Feverroot, Sir Cory Anders Mayapple...."

"But how can that be?" interrupted Linnet. "That book must have been down there for ages."

"Woodwoses are very long-lived," said Moley.

"And a long time ago," continued Hannah, "this part of the forest was completely underwater. Nevermore is all that's left of a very ancient lake. Ships sailed here from other countries, some carried explorers, others carried settlers. Maybe one ran into a storm, a ship that had a woodwose on board, or a whole family of them."

"I don't suppose you'd remember anything like that happening, um …?" Olivier wanted to address the woodwose by his newfound name, but it was such a mouthful. The woodwose had gone straight from having no name to having too many.

"Leafy," he said very quietly and very sadly. "My mother used to call me Leafy."

No one knew what to say, not even Mr. Mirific, who was about to make a wisecrack, then swallowed it with a grimace.

"A bad, bad storm. Terrible. My parents planted me in a lifeboat, about the size of a window box, and set me adrift. 'Be strong, Leafy,' they said, 'and remember who you are.' But I didn't," he sighed.

Olivier touched him gently on the shoulder and said, "You have so many fine names. What should we call you?"

"Leaf," he said simply, wiping a drop of dew from his eyes and brightening. "That's my name."

"Well then, Leaf, how about flipping through that book of yours. I think we're all curious about what's in it."

"Can't. The pages are all stuck together. See?"

"Yeah, hey, they're not stuck, they're just…."

Uncut, cut in Murray. *What you need is a paper knife.*

"A what?"

"A paper knife," groaned Sylvan. "I should have guessed. Of course, *that's* what Dirk is, a knife that's used to slit open the pages of old printed books. That's the way they used to be made, uncut, like a loaf of French bread."

Everyone stared in surprise at Dirk, as if the little dagger had played a trick on them, and indeed its silver blade seemed to flash merrily in the sunlight.

"OK," laughed Olivier, "cut away, Leaf."

He did, and when Dirk had finished slicing open the first few pages no one was much the wiser, for the book was printed in what you might call a natural font — letters that twined and interlaced like branches, stems and vines. Leaf seemed to understand it, though, for he began almost at once to read, slowly at first, then with growing confidence. The title itself was so long, Olivier wondered if it wasn't sprouting and sending out shoots as the woodwose worked his way through it — *Across the Ocean and Into the Trees: Herein the History, Customs, Propagations and Peregrinations of the Woodwose.*

"Bravo," said Linnet. "You must have been a clever sapling to pick up reading so young. And to remember how, after all this time."

"And when you saw yourself in the keyhole of that book," said Olivier, "that was really you, because the book *is* all about you — you and your ancestors."

Leaf looked in amazement from one to the other, then around at the assembled group — the So-So Gang had drifted in from the forest and stood awkwardly on the sidelines. He was so pleased and happy it seemed he might burst into blossom. "I think I'll read more," he said.

"Yes, yes, go ahead," they all urged.

So Leaf sat right down with the book in his lap and gave himself over to a long and absorbing adventure of his very own.

Poe now made an announcement, or maybe it was several, for she began to mew and mew.

"She's full of ideas," said Fathom.

"I hope not," said Olivier, as everyone's attention turned to the Inkling chest upon which she was still sitting. "What's she saying, Murray?"

That it's time for that Mirific fellow — the one you'll notice is sneaking away this very moment — to hand over the key to the chest.

"Another key?"

"Hey, Mirific, get back here!"

"Someone grab him!"

Hard to believe, but it was the So-Sos who tackled the little man and brought him to the ground. Naturally, there was a great deal of hollering on his part and an abundance of curses and complaints, although most of them concerned the grass stains on his white suit. He was duly frisked, the key found — it was tied around his neck — and brought to Olivier.

He was greatly surprised to see *this* key, for it was

the one, or exactly *like* the one, his step-step-step-gramma had pulled out of her pocket when he'd first arrived at Cat's Eye Corner.

"Where did you get this?" he demanded of Mr. Mirific, who in reply only dusted himself off and made a face at Olivier (an accomplishment, as he already *had* quite the face).

"Never mind that," said Linnet. "Try it."

Olivier didn't need much encouragement. The Inklings had fascinated him ever since he first heard about them — and now he'd be able to see what they were actually like. He slid the key into the lock and it turned easily, with a smooth metallic *click*. By this time, Poe had leapt off the chest and was standing beside Bliss. The older cat, as usual, was regarding the proceedings with an impassive, though steady, gaze. Everyone else was very excited.

"C'mon, Olivier."

"Yeah, open it!"

He took a deep breath and flipped open the lid.

"Yes-s-s-s-s-s-s!" He was suddenly overwhelmed by a wave of clambering, fleeing bodies — bodies that were insubstantial, almost transparent, soft as air. Was that a tiny winged horse he saw, that changed into a serpentine Chinese dragon, that turned into a school of silvery fantastic fish, before disappearing altogether?

"How beautiful," sighed Linnet.

"Water music," said Fathom. "Did you hear it?"

"A whole symphony," replied Sylvan.

I believe I have a book in me. Goodness, it's a tight fit.

"A sonnet," stuttered Sputum, in surprise. "I have a sonnet on the tip of my tongue."

If that wasn't alarming enough, Mr. Mirific exclaimed, "I've got an **EXCELLENT** idea!"

"What is it?" asked Olivier, suspiciously.

"My absolutely **STUNNING** and **PROFOUND** idea is that my last idea was **SUPREMELY** stupid! Who would want to change *Great Expectations* to *Greatest Expectations*? Wouldn't be the same now, would it? Who would want to be the **BEST** at everything? That would be boring!"

"I agree," said Olivier, relieved that Mr. Mirific hadn't, under the influence of the liberated Inklings, come up with some new harebrained scheme. "It wouldn't be much fun at all."

This freeing of ideas had certainly sent a creative charge through the gathering and for a short while everyone was chattering at once, suffused with inspiration. Notions were tossed around like balls at a beach party — plans for works of art, scientific theories, plot summaries, musical scores, inventions and even some inspired jokes.

It was Bliss who brought everyone back to earth by making the announcement that Olivier had known would come.

"Meow," he said, peremptorily. Or was it, "Now?"

Bliss was a cat of few mews and when he said it was time to go, it was indeed time. Olivier reluctantly began to say his goodbyes. He shook hands warmly with Linnet, Sylvan, Fathom, the Two Holies, Zeke (a delicate operation, as it would have been awfully gauche to snap off one of his legs) and Leaf, who stopped reading long enough to clasp Olivier's hand gratefully in his own. Olivier even shook hands with every member of the So-So Gang *and* with Mr. Mirific, who this time *did* have a buzzer concealed in his palm — "Haw, haw." Remembering his singed fingers, Olivier bowed to Ashley instead of shaking his paw and the firedog bow-wowed back.

"I'll make sure all the words are properly restored," said Sylvan, holding up a tiny dictionary, a mere seed of a book that, he explained, Wen had saved from being destroyed in the So-So campfire.

"Does that mean we can all have our real names back?" asked Craven. "And our glasses?"

"Darn right," said Wen. "Sure glad I have a second pair."

"Me, too," said Olivier. "We couldn't have done it without you. What *is* your real name?"

"Wendy. The funny thing is, I kind of like Wen better — even if it does mean a sore and a blemish."

Ah, but it is also a variation of the word "wyn," which means "joy."

Wen smiled with pleasure. "Well, Olivier, I'll see you in school. Are you bringing Murray?"

Perish the thought.

"School?"

"Sure. We're the kids nobody notices, remember? You don't think we live here, do you?"

"How did you ... I mean, this is a whole other world, isn't it?"

"I keep telling you it's not," said Linnet, a riff of wind chuckling around Olivier's ear. "It's just an out-of-the-way place."

"Found in a quiet corner," said Hannah.

"Through the Dark Woods," added Moley. "By the way, now that they're back, the Dark Woods that is, you should be careful on your return trip."

"What do you mean?"

"Oh, the usual, nothing much to worry about," said Hannah. "A few wolves."

"Cut-throat bandits, wild boars," added Moley.

"Ghosts."

"Nothing like that comes at the *end* of an adventure," protested Olivier. "Don't you remember that awful creature I had to defeat in the lake? I've met the challenge, I've done that sort of thing already."

"Don't fret," laughed Linnet. "I'll put some wind in your sails and you'll fly through the woods in no time. Say, there go the cats. You'd better follow."

Au revoir. Murray was ready to go.

"Olivier, I forgot to ask what power the blood had. What was it for?"

"For friendship, I think. Or sharing, something like that."

"Not something you really needed then."

"You're a pal, Linnet. Don't forget where to find me, okay? Goodbye, everybody, goodbye."

As everyone began waving and shouting farewell, Linnet raised her hand and soon Olivier felt a rush of air around his feet, feathering his heels. Then he was running and running, fast as the wind, through the Dark and *scary* Woods.

TWENTY

As Olivier ran, skimming past trees and more trees, he was sure he caught sight of more than one ugly mug poking out from between the branches — a highwayman's wicked smile, a desperado's glinting gold tooth. At one point, he saw a pair of green eyes flashing and heard a low menacing growl. These woods *did* seem to be freshly infested with dangers, which made him run even faster, worrying all the while about the cats, for he should have caught up with them by now.

A few times Olivier almost whacked his head on low-lying branches. It wouldn't do to evade all the terrible creatures and spooks here only to knock himself flat out of sheer clumsiness. He tried slowing down — he had developed a painful stitch in his side, anyway — but the moment he did, he sensed he was being followed.

Followed? Make that *chased*. Whatever was approaching, it was swiftly gaining on him, steps thudding on the path, breath rasping. It didn't sound human or animal or like anything he had ever heard before. He didn't even *want* to identify it (not everything deserves a name), he just wanted to escape, so he ran harder and faster than he had ever run before.

Murray was sweating ink in his front pocket. Olivier vowed that no further harm was going to come to his friend on his account and this gave him an extra surge of energy. He picked up speed and ran even *faster*, racing at a side-splitting pace, practically ripping up the path as if it were a dark cloth, as he made his final sprint to Cat's Eye Corner. And there it *was*, finally, looming in the centre of the wood. He shot straight through the orchard, his dreadful pursuer on his heels, getting closer and closer. He could feel its chill presence at his back, its deathly stale breath tumbling like ashes down the neck of his shirt.

The door lay ahead and he hurled himself toward it. Then, for a split second, he stopped cold. Before him was *another* monster, with a glaring and grotesque face, stiff hair encircling its head, tongue protruding, a huge ring through its mouth. The hagoday! A *sanctuary* knocker, that's what Murray had said — it could save your life! Olivier grabbed the ring and immediately there was silence, complete silence. No one, nothing, was behind him now except a faint sulphuric odour in the air, as if the evil at his back had been instantly snuffed out.

"Murray," he gasped. "We're safe! We made it!"

Olivier knew what his sidekick would reply if he could. *Knock, knock, my boy.*

Still holding onto the ring, Olivier lifted and pounded it against the door once, twice, three times. The pounding sounded not like the hollow resounding noise he expected, but more like a heartbeat, the kind of *thud thud thud* you might hear if you put your ear to someone's chest. If this wasn't eerie enough, the door swung open of its own accord to an empty hallway. He didn't recognize it, either. He sure hoped that this was the Cat's Eye Corner where he had started out.

As the only way forward appeared to be up a steep staircase, Olivier followed it. At the top of the landing he discovered yet another closed door. He knocked, tentatively. On the other side, footsteps approached from a distance and then the door sprang open. His step-step-stepgramma stood there against the light, hands raised to her face in surprise.

"Olivier! *Where* have you been?"

"On the scavenger hunt," he replied, matter-of-factly. Had she forgotten? "And I found *everything*."

"Excellent. Come in, come in."

When she ushered him in, Olivier was delighted to find himself in familiar surroundings again. He must have come up the back way, for here was Sylvia's cozy sitting room, complete with comfy chairs, blazing fireplace, steaming pot of tea and *cats*. The Poets were all present and accounted for, including, to his great relief, Bliss and Poe. The tabby, imperturbable as ever, was busy chewing on his toes, while Poe was already curled up fast asleep with her brothers.

"I don't suppose any time has passed at all since I've been gone?" he said, taking a seat by the fire as before.

"On the contrary, my dear," said Sylvia. "You've been missing for days. Your parents have been calling and calling, wanting to speak to you, and I must say it's kept your grandfather and me on our toes just making up stories to tell them. Fortunately, we're very *very* good at making things up." She smiled. "How many sandwiches would you like?"

"Seventeen, please," said Olivier, decisively. When *was* the last time he'd eaten? "You wouldn't happen to have any ink on hand, would you?" He patted his shirtfront pocket. "I'd like to make a few notes, you know, before I forget."

"Certainly, dear. That is a rare writing instrument you have there."

A horrible thought occurred to him. "He's not, I mean, this pen isn't …?"

"Mine? Let's just say, finder's keepers, shall we? Now, eat up and I'll go get your grandfather. You can tell us all about what you've been up to. It's been so dull here without you. We've been playing this silly, endless board game and you'll never guess — it's so peculiar — but we had a flood in one of the upstairs rooms. Imagine! What a mess it made, too."

A flood? Olivier grew thoughtful. "Step-step-step-gramma?"

"Yes?"

"The scavenger hunt was absolutely great, everything you said it would be. But a lot of puzzling things happened."

"Yes ..." This was her opening, her cue to explain everything, as he was certain she could if she wanted. All she did, though, was shake her head and say, "Heavens, don't you find that explanations just ruin a good mystery? Rather like opening a cunningly wrapped present and finding something dreary and disappointing inside — a pair of socks, say."

Olivier *liked* socks. What's wrong with socks? he wanted to ask, but then thought, *What if she gives me a gift some time?* It wouldn't do to sound *too* enthusiastic.

Sylvia then stood abruptly, possibly to avoid further cross-examination about the scavenger hunt, and began slapping at the pockets of her long skirt. "Goodness, what have I done with it?"

"This, you mean?" asked Olivier, pulling from his own pocket the key that he had used to open the Inklings' chest.

"However did you get *that*?"

"Oh," he said, "it's just one of those inexplicable mysteries, I guess." Now it was his turn. "Surely you can tell me," he continued, "why you keep my gramps locked up?"

"It's not *my* idea. He insists that I lock him in his study every day for two hours so he can work on his dictionary. Otherwise, he wouldn't get any work done."

"Dictionary? I didn't know Gramps was writing a *dictionary*."

"Indeed. An immensely important work. Do you know what 'spindlebone' means?"

"No idea."

"Well, then, I'll go fetch the author of the word himself. While you're waiting, *this* might amuse you." Sylvia reached down, slipped her hand behind the seat cushion of her chair and plucked out a ragged and tattered old book, which she handed to him. "I wouldn't want you to get bored," she said as she walked over to the library ladder that was propped against the bookshelves, climbed up and pushed through a trapdoor in the ceiling. Nimbly, she hoisted herself through the opening and disappeared, purple witchy shoes and all. The room was as riddled as swiss cheese with entrances and exits.

Olivier gazed at the book in his hands, wondering how upset Leaf was going to be when he realized he'd lost it. He ran his fingers over the binding — it sure felt the same as the one he had found in Nevermore Lake — but when he opened it, he saw that the title had changed. Rather, it was in the *process* of changing, for the letters on the title page were scurrying around, reorganizing themselves. An "O" popped its top and became a "U," a capital "I" chased a couple of younger, lowercase "i"s into place and an "E" that had been sound asleep and snoring "zzzzzz"s hastily stretched and stood up very straight.

Inklings, he smiled.

The title now read — **E**nquire **W**ithin **U**pon **E**verything.

Wow, he thought, *sounds like my kind of book.* And not only that, it seemed it *was* his book, for these words suddenly appeared below the title — *For Olivier. Tanks a million.*

He couldn't wait to tell Murray. What a great gift — who knew *where* it might lead? Olivier immediately got out Murray and the notebook (it was almost full). He retrieved the scavenger hunt treasures as well and lined them up on the rug in order of their discovery — doily (web), sunstone, skipjack, blood, brain coral, doit, armlet. The hagoday was the only one he'd found and not collected.

"It's funny, Murray, but they don't look very special any more. I bet you anything they've lost their powers now that we're back here. But guess what, it doesn't matter because ... hey, wait a minute, *you're* all right, aren't you? *You* haven't changed, have you?"

He tried to get Murray to say something, but *nothing* happened. He couldn't squeeze a single word out of him. Olivier's heart began to race — *it couldn't be.* Then he spotted a china cup full of ink that Sylvia had already set out on the tea table and he plunged Murray in to see if he could revive him.

Ahhh, a most refreshing libation and in the nick of time, too. I was so empty, I was having writer's cramps.

Olivier laughed and tapped his pal on the cap affectionately. He was about to tell Murray about the book when he noticed Eliot standing by the piano, looking distinguished as usual, which reminded him that it was also time to return the one object that had been particularly helpful. He picked up the sunstone, alias the cat's-eye, took aim and carefully tossed it, so that it landed right in front of Eliot. He stretched out a paw, batted it playfully a few times and then *whapped* it right under the piano. Olivier snorted in surprise, mostly because he thought that Eliot had *winked* at him.

"Murray," he said, "there's no end of surprises here. What's next, d'you think?"

I could write THE END, beautifully, with style, ornate curlicues and all that.

"I don't think it is, though. See what I have here?" Olivier held up the book. "*Very* promising ... and look, the rug is moving. It's lifting up, there's something under it! I better find out what."

I suppose, if you have to.

Olivier folded back the carpet and underneath discovered another trapdoor. This door creaked slowly open, then was thrown back with a loud crash.

"Gramps!"

"Hi, Ollie. By cracky, it's good to see you." The old man climbed up and into the room in order to give his grandson a big hug.

The end, Murray wrote.

"So you want to know what 'spindlebone' means, eh?"

"Yeah, Gramps, I sure do."

The end, the end, the end.

"It has to do with this game I'm making up. It's the goldarnedest, funnest game there is, or will be. Got a list of rules somewhere in my pocket here. Want to try it?"

No! Because it's THE END!!

"Sounds excellent. Why don't you tell me about it and I'll just make a few notes?"

So Gramps plonked himself down in one of the cushy armchairs and began to relate the ins and outs and intriguing undersides of this new game, while Olivier doodled away in his notebook and wrote, to Gramps' great amusement, such things as, *You can't be serious!* and *Count me out!* and *Oh, all right, when do we start?*

ACKNOWLEDGEMENTS

Many thanks to Ethan and Kim Jernigan for reading and commenting so helpfully on an earlier draft of this novel. A special thanks to Sandy Griggs-Burr, who thought up the title, suggested the word "spindlebone" from his own personal dictionary, and is the main reason that the book came to be written. Finally, I would like to thank the Ontario Arts Council for a works-in-progress grant received during the final stage of the writing process.